Margaret Cavendish's The Unnatural Tragedy: A Retelling

David Bruce

Published by David Bruce, 2022.

This is a work of fiction. Similarities to real people, places, or events are entirely coincidental.

MARGARET CAVENDISH'S THE UNNATURAL TRAGEDY: A RETELLING

First edition. September 16, 2022.

Copyright © 2022 David Bruce.

ISBN: 979-8215000977

Written by David Bruce.

Table of Contents

Dedication

Dedicated to My Brother Frank

Frank was reluctant to write the words below, but he did at my request because it's an opportunity to show that people still do good deeds. This can help restore people's faith in humanity.

"I've put some thought into this, and here a few Good Deeds I've done.

"I've bought breakfast more than once for complete strangers at my favorite local diner (Tommy's Diner) just because they looked like they could use a free meal.

"A woman came into Tommy's Diner, looking like she could use a decent meal and would appreciate it being free. I watched as she walked through the restaurant and sat down. I thought to myself, 'Buy her lunch.' I fought the urge and told myself no. I looked at her after she ordered and received her meal and thought to myself, 'Buy her lunch.' Again, I told myself no. She is a complete stranger, and money is hard to come by for me as well as everyone else. I was in line at the check-out waiting to pay my bill. She came up and got into line behind me and I thought to myself, 'Buy her lunch!' I looked at her, she looked at me, I reached out and grabbed her ticket, but she didn't want to let go. I told her sort of sternly, 'I don't know why, but I really, really want to pay for your lunch. I know we are complete strangers, but I feel like I am supposed to pay for your lunch. Will you please give me the pleasure of paying for this?' She almost cried, but she did allow me the pleasure.

"In Columbus, Ohio, almost always someone is at the gas station wanting money. One day this guy asked for money. I asked him, 'Why do you want money?' He said he's hungry. (If you don't know, Speedway has hotdogs and other food and drink items.) I said, 'Come inside, I'll buy you something to eat.' He was a really nice guy. His name was Dave, and he was an Army veteran; he may have been a little mentally ill after serving in the military. He talked to me about the war (don't know what war) and how he was over there fighting bulldozers. I think a couple of hotdogs and a hot coffee made his day. It really put a smile on his face. I ended up liking this guy and I'd look for him when I was getting gas so I could help him out.

"One time a guy came in the restaurant selling an old leather jacket for $10.00 so he could get some gas. It didn't fit me, and I didn't want it anyway, but I bought it and then donated the jacket.

"A woman was driving her car with the alarm going off, so I helped her figure out how to turn it off. She had the key fob, so I'm sure she didn't steal the car.

"These are a few of the good deeds I've had the pleasure of doing."
***

The doing of good deeds is important. As a free person, you can choose to live your life as a good person or as a bad person. To be a good person, do good deeds. To be a bad person, do bad deeds. If you do good deeds, you will become good. If you do bad deeds, you will become bad. To become the person you want to be, act as if you already are that kind of person. Each of us chooses what kind of person we will become. To become a good person, do the things a good person does. To become a bad person, do the things a bad person does. The opportunity to take action to become the kind of person you want to be is yours.

Human beings have free will. According to the Babylonian Niddah 16b, whenever a baby is to be conceived, the Lailah (angel in charge of contraception) takes the drop of semen that will result in the conception and asks God, "Sovereign of the Universe, what is going to be the fate of this drop? Will it develop into a robust or into a weak person? An intelligent or a stupid person? A wealthy or a poor person?" The Lailah asks all these questions, but it does not ask, "Will it develop into a righteous or a wicked person?" The answer to that question lies in the decisions to be freely made by the human being that is the result of the conception.

A Buddhist monk visiting a class wrote this on the chalkboard: "EVERYONE WANTS TO SAVE THE WORLD, BUT NO ONE WANTS TO HELP MOM DO THE DISHES." The students laughed, but the monk then said, "Statistically, it's highly unlikely that any of you will ever have the opportunity to run into a burning orphanage and rescue an infant. But, in the smallest gesture of kindness — a warm smile, holding the door for the person behind you, shoveling the driveway of the elderly person next door — you have committed an act of immeasurable profundity, because to each of us, our life is our universe."

In her book titled I HAVE CHOSEN TO STAY AND FIGHT, comedian Margaret Cho writes, "I believe that we get complimentary snack-size portions of the afterlife, and we all receive them in a different way." For Ms. Cho, many of her snack-size portions of the afterlife come in hip hop music. Other people get different snack-size portions of the afterlife, and we all must be on the lookout for them when they come our way. And perhaps doing good deeds and experiencing good deeds are snack-size portions of the afterlife.

Educate Yourself
Read Like a Wolf Eats
Be Excellent to Each Other
Books Then, Books Now, Books Forever

***

In this retelling, as in all my retellings, I have tried to make the work of literature accessible to modern readers who may lack some of the knowledge about mythology, religion, and history that the literary work's contemporary audience had.

Do you know a language other than English? If you do, I give you permission to translate this book, copyright your translation, publish or self-publish it, and keep all the royalties for yourself. (Do give me credit, of course, for the original retelling.)

I would like to see my retellings of classic literature used in schools, so I give permission to the country of Finland (and all other countries) to give copies of any or all of my retellings to all students forever. I also give permission to the state of Texas (and all other states) to give copies of this book to all students forever. I also give permission to all teachers to give copies of this book to all students forever.

Teachers need not actually teach my retellings. Teachers are welcome to give students copies of my eBooks as background material. For example, if they are teaching Homer's *Iliad* and *Odyssey*, teachers are welcome to give students copies of my *Virgil's* Aeneid: *A Retelling in Prose* and tell students, "Here's another ancient epic you may want to read in your spare time."

CAST OF CHARACTERS

Monsieur FRERE. *Frere* means BROTHER.

Madame SOEUR (sister of FRERE). *Soeur* means SISTER.

Monsieur PERE (father of FRERE and SOEUR). *Pere* means FATHER.

Monsieur MARI (husband of SOEUR). *Mari* means HUSBAND.

Mademoiselle AMOUR (engaged to FRERE). *Amour* means LOVE.

Monsieur SENSIBLE (father of Mademoiselle AMOUR).

Monsieur MALATESTE. Malateste can mean BADLY TESTED, BAD TESTER, or BAD MAN (BAD TESTICLE).

Madame BONIT (first wife of Monsieur MALATESTE). BONIT means GOOD.

Monsieur FEFY (friend of Monsieur MALATESTE).

The sociable VIRGINS

First VIRGIN (later MADAME MALATESTE, second wife of MONSIEUR MALATESTE)

Second VIRGIN

Third VIRGIN

Fourth VIRGIN

Fifth VIRGIN. The fifth virgin may be shy and/or younger than the other virgins because she speaks much less than the other virgins. When they take turns rhyming, she rhymes two lines while the other virgins rhyme four lines.

MATRONS (chaperones to the sociable VIRGINS)

First MATRON
Second MATRON

Malateste household staff

NAN
JOAN
MAIDS
SERVANTS
STEWARD
FRIEND (of Monsieur FRERE).
MAN (servant to Monsieur FRERE).

First GENTLEMAN
Second GENTLEMAN
NOTES:
Andrew Duxfield, now of the University Of Liverpool, edited this play and provided an excellent introduction and notes.
https://extra.shu.ac.uk/emls/iemls/renplays/The%20Unnatural%20Tragedy.pdf
This play has three plots:

1) Monsieur FRERE pursues an incestuous relationship with his sister, Madame SOEUR.

2) The sociable VIRGINS discuss intellectual and social topics.

3) Monsieur MALATESTE, who is married to Madame BONIT, is pursuing an affair with the maid NAN.

The Unnatural Tragedy was first published in Margaret Cavendish's 1662 book titled *Plays*.

John Ford's play *'Tis Pity She's a Whore* also has a plot involving incest.

Doctors in Margaret Cavendish's society believed that the human body had four humors, or vital fluids, that determined one's temperament. Each humor made a contribution to the personality, and one humor could be predominant. For a human being to be sane and healthy, the four humors had to be present in the right amounts. If a man had too much of a certain humor, it would harm his personality and health.

Blood was the sanguine humor. A sanguine man was optimistic.

Phlegm was the phlegmatic humor. A phlegmatic man was calm.

Yellow bile was the choleric humor. A choleric man was angry.

Black bile was the melancholic humor. A melancholic man was gloomy.

A humor can be a personal characteristic.

A humor can also be a fancy or a whim or a mood.

In this society, a person of higher rank would use "thou," "thee," "thine," and "thy" when referring to a person of lower rank. (These terms were also used affectionately and between equals.) A person of lower rank would use "you" and "your" when referring to a person of higher rank.

The word "wench" in this society was not necessarily negative. It was often used affectionately.

The word "wit" in this society means "intelligence."

YouTube Video

The Unnatural Tragedy (1662) by Margaret Cavendish

It is an online expressive reading of the play with many Indian actors taking part. The language spoken is English.

"Jan 21, 2021. One of the greatest plays ever written and the 'missing link' between Jacobean and Restoration theatre. The form is remarkable and the content, although often hilarious, touches on issues such as incest, rape, the emotional abuse of women, and suicide. It's by no means heavy going but really accessible and totally speaks to a 21st Century audience."

https://www.youtube.com/watch?v=8MPv_bJEEH0

YouTube CHANNEL: Lost Ladies of Theater (Found)

https://www.youtube.com/channel/UCCMcnC-qP5Qagxt-k1VFrig

PROLOGUE

A tragedy I usher in today;

    All mirth is banished in this serious play.

    Yet sad contentment may she to you bring,

    In pleased expressions of each several [different] thing.

    Our poetess is confident, nor fears,

    Though 'gainst her sex the tragic buskins wears,

    But you will like it. Some few hours spent,

    She'll know your censure [judgment of the play] by your hands [applause, or lack of it] what's meant.

This prologue was written by the Lord Marquess of Newcastle.

Notes:

Buskins were shoes used in tragedies. They had thick soles to give the tragic actor additional height.

The Lord Marquess of Newcastle is William Cavendish, the husband of Margaret Cavendish.

CHAPTER 1

— 1.1 —

Monsieur Frere and his friend talked together. They were young Frenchmen who had been traveling together, and they were currently in Venice.

"Since we have come out of our own country to travel, we will go into Turkey, if you will, and see that country," Monsieur Frere said.

The friend replied:

"With all my heart.

"But now that I think better about it, I will stay here a while longer for the courtesans' sake, for we shall never get such an abundance, nor such a choice of mistresses. For although the sober and chaste women are kept hidden away up here in Italy, yet the wild and wanton women are let loose to take their liberty."

The word "courtesan" means "court-mistress."

Euphemistically, "courtesan" means "prostitute."

The friend continued:

"But in Turkey, that barbarous country, all are kept hidden away: those who would as well as those who would not.

"But if they had the custom of Italy — to keep shut away only their honest women — it would be a charity, for otherwise a man loses his time in courting those women who will not accept his love. For how should a man know whether women will or will not, when all the women have sober faces and demure countenances, coy — that is, shy — body language and denying words?"

Honest women are chaste women.

"But yet they consent eventually," Monsieur Frere said, "for importunity and opportunity, it is said, wins the chastest she."

In other words, if the man is persistent and has a good opportunity, even the chastest woman will submit to his love or his "love."

This has been said about many women, including Ulysses' wife, Penelope, who remained chaste during the twenty years that her husband spent away from home. The first ten years he spent fighting the Trojan War, and the second ten years he spent trying to get back home. Much of that time he was kept captive on an island by the goddess Calypso.

5

During much of that time, people assumed that Ulysses was dead, and over 100 suitors tried to convince Penelope to marry one of them. Penelope was able to hold them off for some time with her famous weaving trick. She told them that after she had woven a shroud for Ulysses' father, Laertes, she would choose one of them to marry. Each day she wove the shroud, and each night she unwove what she had woven.

Monsieur Frere's friend replied:

"Indeed, all the flowery rhetoric, and the most observing times, and fittest opportunities, and counterfeiting dyings win nothing upon a cold, icy constitution or an obstinate morality."

He was saying that seduction techniques such as claiming that one will die if one's love is not returned don't work on women with a cold, icy character or a resolute sense of morality.

While Italian soprano Luisa Tetrazzini (1871-1940) was living in Argentina, where she was very popular, the 20-year-old son of her host fell in love with her. He appeared before her, holding a silver-handled dagger and threatening to kill himself if she did not kiss him. She replied, "We Italians never kiss anyone unless we know them very well. Now suppose you give me that lovely dagger of yours, then I will go out on the lawn and tell you presently [soon] if I like you well enough to kiss you." Her playing for time worked. She did not have to give the young man a kiss, but she did acquire a silver-handled dagger that she used for the next 15 years while singing in the opera *Lucia di Lammermoor*.

The friend continued:

"It is true that it may work some good effect upon an icy conscience."

In other words: Seduction techniques may work when used on a woman whose inner thoughts are initially unfriendly toward the man, but whose thoughts potentially can be changed, unlike those of a woman with a persistent cold, icy character. Flowery persuasiveness and persistence may change the woman's mind.

A serving-man entered the room, carrying a letter for Monsieur Frere.

"From whence comes that letter?" Monsieur Frere asked.

The serving-man gave Monsieur Frere the letter and answered, "From France, sir. I believe that it comes from your father."

Monsieur Frere opened the letter and read it to himself.

"What is the news?" his friend asked. "Has thy father sent thee money?"

"Yes, but it is to be used for my return home," Monsieur Frere said, "for he has sent me word that my sister has been married to a very rich, honest, and sweet-natured man, and that also he would have me come to marry a rich heir, one who is his neighbor's daughter. For my father says he desires to see me settled in the world before he dies, having only us two, my sister and me, as his children."

This society had arranged marriages. Parents would try to arrange for their children marriages that would bring wealth and social status to the family.

"Why? Is he sick?" the friend asked. "Is that why he talks about dying?"

"No, but he is old," Monsieur Frere said, "and old age is more certain of death's approach than illness is."

"But do you say that your sister is married?" the friend asked.

"Yes," Monsieur Frere said.

"Indeed, I am sorry for it, for I thought to have married her myself," the friend said.

"By the Virgin, she would have had but a wild husband if she had you," Monsieur Frere said.

The Virgin is the Virgin Mary, mother of Jesus.

"The thoughts of this rich heir make thee speak most precisely, as if thou were the most temperate man in the world, when there is none so deboist — so debauched — as thou are," the friend said.

Monsieur Frere had an unsavory reputation among those who knew him.

"Please hold thy tongue, for I am very discreet," Monsieur Frere said.

"Yes, you are discreet when it comes to hiding thy faults, to dissembling thy passions, and to achieving thy desires, but not to abating and lessening any of them," the friend said. "Well, if thy sister had not been married, I would have praised thee, but now I will rail against thee; for losers may have permission to talk."

He had lost the chance to marry Monsieur Frere's sister.

"Why, what hopes could you have had to marry her?" Monsieur Frere asked.

"Why, I was thy friend, and that was hope enough," the friend said. "But is thy sister as beautiful as gossip reports her to be?"

Monsieur Frere said:

"I cannot tell, for I have never seen her since I was a little boy and she was a very young child.

"I was kept strictly at boarding school and from there I went to the university. And, when I was to travel, I went home, but then she was at an aunt's house a hundred miles from my father's house, and so I didn't see her.

"But I must leave off this discourse, unless you'll return to France with me."

"No, indeed, thou shall return without me, for I would not go so soon unless my friends had provided me a rich heiress to welcome me home," the friend said. "But, since they have not, I mean to stay and entertain myself and spend time with the plump Venetians."

In some cultures, plumpness is seen as very attractive.

Monsieur Frere said, "Fare thee well, friend, and take heed you don't contract a disease."

Venereal disease was a possible illness that could be contracted while pursuing the kind of entertainment these two young men pursued.

The friend joked:

"Thou speak as if thou were a *Convertito*."

Convertito is Italian for "religious convert."

— 1.2 —

Madame Bonit, alone, was sitting down to work at sewing. As she was working, Monsieur Malateste, her husband, entered the room.

"You are always at work!" Monsieur Malateste said. "What use is it? You spend more money in silk, crewel, thread, and the like than all your work is worth."

Crewel was a type of yarn that was used while embroidering and in creating tapestries.

"I am now making you bands," Madame Bonit said.

She was making decorative collars for her husband.

"Please let my bands alone, for I'm sure they will be so ill-favored that I cannot wear them," Monsieur Malateste said.

"Ill-favored" can mean ugly in appearance.

Monsieur Malateste was ugly in his treatment of his wife.

"Do not condemn them before you have tried them," Madame Bonit said.

"You may make them, but I will never wear them," Monsieur Malateste said.

"Well, I will not make them, since you dislike it," Madame Bonit said.

Two gentlemen talked together.

"Come, will you go to the gaming-house?" the first gentleman asked.

"To do what?" the second gentleman asked.

Gambling occurred there.

"To play at cards, or the like games," the first gentleman answered.

"I will never play at such games except with women," the second gentleman said.

"Why so?" the first gentleman asked.

"Because they are effeminate pastimes, and not manly actions," the second gentleman said. "Neither will I merely rely upon Fortune's favor without merit, as gamesters do."

In gambling, a bad person can draw a game-winning card.

"Will you then go to a tavern?" the first gentleman asked.

"Why?" the second gentleman said.

"To drink," the first gentleman answered.

"I am not thirsty," the second gentleman said.

"But I would have you drink until you are thirsty, " the first gentleman said.

Drinking alcohol can dehydrate a person.

"That's to drink drunk," the second gentleman said.

"And that's what I desire to be," the first gentleman said.

"What?" the second gentleman asked.

"Why, drunk," the first gentleman said.

The second gentleman said:

"I do not wish to be drunk because I will not willfully make myself incapable with the result that I am not able to serve my king, my country, or my friend, and I am not able to defend my honor, for when I am drunk, I can do none of these things.

Charles II was King of England in 1662, when *The Unnatural Tragedy* was published.

The second gentleman continued:

"A man who is drunk is weaker than a child who hasn't the strength to walk or stand, and he is worse than those who are incapable of speech because the dumb keep silent, whereas those who are drunk stutter and stammer out nonsense and make themselves fools.

"Besides, every coward will take courage to beat — or at least affront — a man who is drunk, whereas he does not dare to look askew or come near him without respect when he is sober."

"Come, come," the first gentleman said. "Thou shall go, if only to decide our drunken quarrels and allay the wrathful vapor of Bacchus."

The second gentlemen could stay sober and act as a judge in the drunken quarrels of others.

In this context, vapors are moods.

Bacchus is the god of wine and pleasure. Euripides' *Bacchae* makes it clear that proper attention must be paid to this god lest he take revenge. If the second gentleman will not drink, then at least he can be around those who do.

Bacchus is not Christian. Christianity regards gluttony — habitually overindulging in food or drink — as one of the Seven Deadly Sins: Pride, Envy, Gluttony, Lust, Anger (Wrath), Greed (Avarice or Covetousness), and Sloth.

In Dante's *Inferno*, the unrepentant gluttons are punished in the Third Circle. Mud is plentiful in the third Circle of the Inferno because rain is always falling. The Gluttons wanted to enjoy the good things of life, but now they are forced to live in uncomfortable surroundings — surroundings much like a muddy pigsty. The Gluttons made pigs of themselves while living, and now, although they are dead, they live like pigs. Dante the Pilgrim speaks briefly with a Florentine Glutton named Ciacco — a nickname that means "pig" or "hog." After their brief conversation, Ciacco lies down and goes to sleep in a stupor in the mud, just like a glutton would go to sleep in a stupor after enjoying a huge meal.

Since Bacchus is the god of pleasure as well as of wine, he may advocate that non-alcoholics drink wine in moderation.

"No, I will never decide the disputes of fools, madmen, drunkards, or women," the second gentleman said, "for fools understand no reason, madmen have lost their reason, drunkards will hear no reason, and women are not capable of reason."

"Why aren't women capable of reason?" the first gentleman asked.

"Because it is thought — or rather believed — that women have no rational souls, being created out of man, and not from Jove, as man was," the second gentleman said.

Adam was directly created by God, and then God used one of Adam's ribs to create Eve.

Jove is Jupiter, king of the gods. The name "Jove" is sometimes used in Elizabethan, Jacobean, and Carolinian plays to mean the Judeo-Christian God.

Genesis 22-24 states (King James Version):

22 And the rib, which the Lord God had taken from man, made he a woman, and brought her unto the man.

23 And Adam said, This is now bone of my bones, and flesh of my flesh: she shall be called Woman, because she was taken out of Man.

24 Therefore shall a man leave his father and his mother, and shall cleave unto his wife: and they shall be one flesh.

"If Jove hasn't given them rational souls, I am sure that nature has given them beautiful bodies with which Jove is enamored, or else the poets lie," the first gentleman said.

Jove had affairs with many immortal goddesses and mortal women.

"Poets describe Jove according to their own passions and after their own appetites," the second gentleman said.

In other words: Poets create Jove in their own image.

"Poets are Jove's priests," the first gentleman said.

"And nature's panders," the second gentleman said.

Poets are nature's panders because they write love poetry. Such poetry can arouse feelings of love — and lust. See Andrew Marvell's "To His Coy [Shy] Mistress" and Robert Herrick's "To the Virgins, To Make Much of Time."

Such poets make good wingmen.

A pander is a pimp.

"Well, if you will not go to the gaming-house, tavern, or bawdy-house, will you go and visit the sociable virgins?" the first gentleman asked.

Virgins are young, unmarried women who are assumed to be chaste.

"Yes, I like sociable virginity very well," the second gentleman said. "But please, who are those sociable virgins whom you would have me go to see?"

"Why, they are a company of young ladies who meet every day to discourse and talk, to examine, to form opinions, and to judge everybody and everything," the first gentleman said.

"It's a pity if they have not learned the rules of logic, if they talk so much," the second gentleman said. They need to know the rules of logic so that they may talk sense."

"I assure you they have voluble — quick and ready — tongues and quick wits," the first gentleman said. "Let us go then."

They exited.

— 1.4 —

Monsieur Malateste said his wife, Madame Bonit, "Lord, how badly you are dressed today!"

"Why, I am chastely dressed," Madame Bonit replied.

"You need to be chastely dressed, for if you were badly dressed and sluttish, too, you could not be endured," Monsieur Malateste said.

"Well, husband, I will strive to be more fashionably dressed," Madame Bonit said.

— 1.5 —

Monsieur Pere talked to his son, Monsieur Frere, who had just returned from his travels.

"Well, son, except that you are like a stranger — I have not seen you in a long time — I would otherwise have rebuked you for spending so much money since you began to travel," Monsieur Pere said.

"Sir, travelling is expensive, especially when a man goes to inform himself about the fashions, manners, customs, and countries he travels through," Monsieur Frere said.

And inform himself about the courtesans.

Madame la Soeur and Monsieur Mari, her husband, greeted and welcomed their brother home.

"Look, son," Monsieur Pere said. "I have increased the size of my family since you went from home: Your sister's beauty has gotten me another son."

Monsieur Mari had become Monsieur Pere's son-in-law.

"And I make no question but my brother's noble and gallant actions will get you another daughter," Madame la Soeur said.

When Monsieur Frere married, Monsieur Pere would gain a daughter-in-law.

"Well, son, I must have you make haste and marry so that you may give me some grandchildren to uphold my posterity, for I have only you two biological children," Monsieur Pere said, "and your sister, I hope, will bring me a grandson soon, for her maids say that she is sick in the mornings, which is a good sign that she is pregnant, although she will not confess it. For young married wives are ashamed to confess when they are with child; they keep it as private as if their child were unlawfully begotten."

One reason to keep it secret is that many pregnancies end with a miscarriage. Among women who know that they are pregnant, about one woman in eight will miscarry.

During this conversation, Monsieur Frere had stared at his sister.

"I think my brother somewhat resembles my wife," Monsieur Mari said.

"No, surely not, brother," Monsieur Frere said. "So unrefined a face as mine can never resemble such a well-shaped face as my sister's."

"I believe the Venetian ladies had a better opinion of your face and body than you deliver of yourself," Monsieur Mari said.

"My brother cannot choose but be weary, coming so long a journey today," Madame la Soeur said. "Therefore it is fitting that we should permit him to pull off his boots."

"Son, now that I think about it, I fear that you have grown so tender since you went into Italy that you can hardly endure having your boots roughly pulled off," Monsieur Pere said.

"I am very sound, sir, and in very good health," Monsieur Frere said.

"Are thou?" Monsieur Pere said. "Come this way, then."

They exited.

— 1.6 —

Monsieur Malateste said to Madame Bonit, "Wife, I have some occasion to sell some land, and I have none that is so convenient to sell as your jointure."

The purpose of a jointure is to provide financial security to a wife if her husband were to die first. It was the portion of her husband's estate that would support her if she became a widow.

"All my friends will condemn me as a fool if I should part with my jointure," Madame Bonit said.

"Why, then you will not part with it?" Monsieur Malateste asked.

Madame Bonit began, "I do not say so; for I think you are so honest a man that if you should die before me, as Heaven forbid you should —"

Monsieur Malateste interrupted, "— nay, stop your prayers."

"Well, husband, you shall have my jointure," Madame Bonit said.

"If I shall, go fetch it," Monsieur Malateste said.

She went out, and then returned, bringing the relevant document and gave it to him. He made haste to leave her.

"Surely, husband, I deserve a kiss for it," Madame Bonit said.

"I cannot stay to kiss," Monsieur Malateste said.

He exited.

Madame Bonit's maid, Joan, entered the room.

"Madam, what will you have for your supper?" Joan asked. "For I hear my master will not eat at home."

"Anything, Joan," Madame Bonit said, "a little ponado, or water-gruel."

Ponado, aka panada, is a kind of soup made by boiling bread to a pulp in water. The soup can be flavored and/or spiced.

Water-gruel is oatmeal boiled in water.

Both are simple, humble, inexpensive foods.

"Your ladyship's diet is not costly," Joan said.

"It satisfies nature as well as costly olios or bisques," Madame Bonit said, "and I desire only to feed my hunger, not my taste; for I am neither gluttonous nor lickerish."

Olios are many-ingredient stews made with spiced meats and vegetables.

Bisques are rich soups made with seafood.

A lickerish person is fond of delicious food.

"No, I'll be sworn you are not," Joan said.

— 1.7 —

The five sociable virgins and the two grave matrons met together.

"Come ladies, what topic of discourse shall we have today?" the first matron asked.

"Let us sit and rail against — vigorously complain about — men," the first virgin said.

Hmm. At first meeting, it seems that the five sociable virgins will fail Allison Bechtel's test.

According to the Wikipedia article titled "Bechtel test," "*The Bechdel test is a measure of the representation of women in fiction. It asks whether a work features at least two women who talk to each other about something other than a man. The requirement that the two women be named is sometimes added.*"

None of the five sociable virgins are ever named, but they will talk about things other than men.

"I know that young ladies love men too well to rail against them," the second matron said. "Besides, men always praise the effeminate sex, and will you rail at those who praise you?"

"Though men praise us before our faces, they rail at us behind our backs," the second virgin said.

"That's when you are unkind or cruel," the second matron said.

"No, it is when we have been too kind and they have taken a surfeit of — been too much in — our company," the third virgin said.

"Indeed, an over-plus — a surplus — of kindness will soon surfeit a man's affection," the first matron said.

"To surfeit" means "to get enough" or "to get too much."

"Therefore I hate them, and I resolve to live a single life," the fourth virgin said, "and I hate men so much, that if the power of Alexander the Great and Julius Caesar were joined into one arm, and the courage of Achilles and Hector were joined into one heart, and the wisdom of Solomon and Ulysses were joined into one brain, and the eloquence of Tully and Demosthenes were joined into one tongue, and all of these things were joined into and made one man, and this man had the beauty of Narcissus, and the youth of Adonis, and would marry me, I would not marry him."

The sociable virgins were well educated.

Alexander the Great was a Macedonian who conquered all the world that was known to the ancient Greeks.

Alexander the Great heard about Diogenes, a Cynic philosopher who lived simply and rejected materialism. While in Athens, Alexander met him and asked if he could do anything for him. In doing so, Alexander stood between the famous Cynic and the sun and cast a shadow on him. Diogenes replied, "Yes, you can stand out of my sunlight."

Alexander told him, "If I were not Alexander, I would want to be Diogenes." Diogenes replied, "If I were not Diogenes, I would want to be Diogenes."

When Alexander wondered why Diogenes was looking at a pile of bones, Diogenes replied, "I am looking for the bones of your father, but I cannot distinguish them from the bones of his slaves."

Julius Caesar was a Roman general who fought and won a civil war against his rival, Pompey, and who became Dictator of Rome.

During the Roman civil wars when Julius Caesar fought Gnaeus Pompeius Magnus — Pompey the Great — for power, Julius Caesar landed on the coast of north Africa. As he jumped from his ship into the shallow water, he stumbled and fell. Knowing that his superstitious Roman troops regarded accidental stumbling as an unlucky omen, Julius Caesar pretended that he had not stumbled. He grabbed two fistfuls of sand, stood up, and raised his hands so his troops could see the sand. He then yelled, "Africa, I hold you in my hands!" Hearing these inspiring words, his troops charged upon the beach with high morale.

Achilles, a Greek man, was the greatest warrior in the Trojan War. When Agamemnon, leader of the Greek forces against Troy, insulted him, Achilles and his soldiers stopped fighting the Trojans, with disastrous results.

Hector was the greatest Trojan warrior in the Trojan War. In Book 6 of Homer's *Iliad*, Hector returned to Troy to ask his mother and the older Trojan women to pray to the goddess Athena. He then visited his wife, Andromache, and his young son. His son was scared by Hector's helmet and screamed until Hector took it off. Andromache smiled through her tears. After Troy fell, a Greek warrior wearing a helmet killed Hector's young son by throwing him down from the high walls of Troy.

Solomon was a wise Old Testament leader. The Judgment of Solomon, a tale that illustrates his wisdom, is told in 1 Kings 3:16-28. Two women disputed about who was the mother of a baby boy. Solomon ordered that a sword be brought to cut the infant in half so that each woman could share the boy (King James Version):

24 And the king said, Bring me a sword. And they brought a sword before the king.

25 And the king said, Divide the living child in two, and give half to the one, and half to the other.

26 Then spake the woman whose the living child was unto the king, for her bowels yearned upon her son, and she said, O my lord, give her the living child, and in no wise slay it. But the other said, Let it be neither mine nor thine, but divide it.

27 Then the king answered and said, Give her the living child, and in no wise slay it: she is the mother thereof.

28 And all Israel heard of the judgment which the king had judged; and they feared the king: for they saw that the wisdom of God was in him, to do judgment.

All Israel *feared* Solomon: This means that they were awed by him and felt reverence for him and did his will.

Ulysses was a wise warrior of the Trojan War. He thought up the idea of the Trojan Horse, a trick that led to the fall of Troy after ten years of war.

Marcus Tullius Cicero was a famous Roman orator. Cicero was also a lawyer and defended a man named Milo, who was accused of killing the infamous aristocrat Clodius. The prosecution asked Cicero, "What time did Clodius die?" Cicero answered, "*Sero,*" which means both "late" and "too late." In other words, Clodius died late in the morning, but he should have died a long time ago.

Demosthenes was a famous ancient Greek orator. Suffering from stuttering, he worked hard to overcome this impediment by putting pebbles in his mouth to slow his speech and force himself to enunciate each syllable clearly.

Narcissus was so handsome that he fell in love with his own reflection in a pool of water. He stared at his reflection and didn't stop even to eat. Eventually, he wasted away and died. After his death, the narcissus flower appeared.

Adonis was a young man whom Venus, goddess of sexual passion, loved. He died while hunting after being gored by a boar. His red blood and Venus' tears mingled and anemone flowers grew into existence.

Narcissus and Adonis are mythological characters. The others are historical.

"Lady, let me tell you, the youth and beauty would tempt you much," the second matron said.

"You are deceived," the fourth virgin said. "For if I would marry, I would sooner marry one who was old in years, for it would be better to choose grave age than fantastical, irrational youth. Nevertheless, I will never marry. For those who are unmarried appear like birds, full of life and spirit; but those who are married appear like beasts, dull and heavy, especially married men."

"Men never appear like beasts except when women make them so," the first matron said.

"They deserve to be made beasts when they strive to make women fools," the first virgin said.

"Nay, they think that we are fools rather than make us so," the second virgin said, "for most husbands think, when their wives are good and obedient, that they are simple."

"When I am married, I'll never give my husband cause to think me simple for my obedience because I will be cross enough," the first virgin said.

Clearly, the first virgin believed that she would be cross to her husband when she becomes a wife.

The third virgin said:

"That's the best way to be.

"For husbands think a cross and contradicting wife is intelligent, a bold and commanding wife has a heroic spirit, a cunning and tricky wife is wise, a prodigal wife is generous, a false wife is beautiful, and he loves her best for those good qualities that if he did not love her he would hate her for."

In other words: The qualities that a husband loves in his wife are the same qualities that he would hate if he did not love her.

Often, things that are cute in the other person early in a relationship become irritating later.

A marriage may seem ideal to people who see it from the outside, but after the marriage breaks up, those on the inside often talk about how unhappy they were.

The third virgin concluded:

"Indeed, the falser she is, the fonder he is of her."

The word "fond" can mean "foolish."

"Nay," the fourth virgin said, "with your permission, let me say that for the most part wives are so enslaved that they dare not look upon any men except their husbands."

"What better object can a woman have than her husband?" the first matron asked.

The first virgin said:

"With your permission, matron, one object is tiresome to view often, while a variety of objects are very pleasing and delightful to view because a variety of objects clear the senses and refresh the mind, while viewing only one object dulls both sense and mind.

"This is why married wives are so sad and melancholy when they keep no other company but their husbands. And, in truth, they have reason for being sad and melancholy; for a husband is a surfeit to the eyes, which causes a loathing dislike in the mind.

"And the truth is that variety is the life and delight of Nature's works, and women — being the only daughters of Nature, and not the sons of Jove, as men are feigned to be — are more pleased with variety than men are."

Jove is Jupiter, king of the gods and men. Sometimes, as in this play, "Jove" can mean "God."

"Which is no honor to the effeminate sex," the first matron said. "But I perceive, lady, you are a true begotten daughter of Mother Nature, and you will follow the steps of your mother."

"Yes, or else I should be unnatural, which I will never be," the first virgin said.

Clearly, the first virgin believed that she would seek a variety of objects other than her husband to look at when she becomes a wife.

CHAPTER 2

— 2.1 —

Monsieur Pere and Monsieur Frere talked together.

"Sir, I wonder, since my sister is so beautiful, why you did not marry her more to her advantage," Monsieur Frere said to his father.

"Why, son, I think I have married her very well for your advantage," Monsieur Pere said, "for her beauty was her only portion, and she is married to a noble gentleman who has a very great estate."

Madame Soeur had no marriage portion — no dowry — other than her beauty. This meant that Monsieur Frere would inherit more wealth.

"But sir, her beauty deserves a king, nay, an emperor: a Caesar of the world," Monsieur Frere said.

"O, son, you are young, which makes you partial on your sister's side," Monsieur Pere said.

— 2.2 —

Madame Bonit criticized her maid, Nan: "It's a strange forgetfulness not to come near me in two hours but let me sit all that time without a fire. If you were my mistress, I should make it a matter of conscience to be more diligent than you are, if I took wages for my service as you do."

"If you do not like me, hire another maid," Nan said.

"If you are weary of my service, please change your employer," Madame Bonit said. "Perhaps you may get a better mistress, and I hope I shall get as careful a servant to take care of me."

A mistress in this sense is a female boss.

— 2.3 —

The five sociable virgins and the two grave matrons met together.

The first virgin said:

"I would have all women educated to manage civil affairs and men to manage the military, both by sea and by land.

"Also, I would have the women educated to follow all manufactures at home and the men educated to follow all affairs that are abroad.

"Likewise, the men would be employed in all arts of labor, and the women would be employed in all arts of curiosity."

Two meanings of "curiosity," according to the *Oxford English Dictionary*, are 1) "careful attention to detail," and 2) "Desire to know or learn."

The arts of curiosity include science.

This world needs good brains. If women's brains are ignored, the world is wasting half of the human brains on this planet.

"Certainly, if women were employed in the affairs of state, the world would live more happily," the second virgin said.

"As long as they were employed in those things or business that were proper for their strength and capacity," the third virgin said.

"Let me tell you, ladies, women have no more capacity than what is as thin as a cobweb lawn, which every eye may see through, even those that are weak and half blind," the first matron said.

Cobweb lawn is a fine, transparent fabric.

"Why, we are not fools," the fourth virgin said. "We are capable of knowledge; we only need experience and education to make us as wise as men."

"But women are incapable of public employments," a matron said.

"Some, we will grant, are; so are some men," the first virgin said. "For some are not made fit to be statesmen by Heaven, by nature, or by education."

The second virgin said:

"And education is the chief, for lawyers and divines can never be good statesmen for these reasons:

"They are too learned to be wise.

"They may be good orators, but never subtle — cunning — counselors.

"They are better disputers than contrivers.

"They are fitter for faction than reformation: The one makes quarrels, or upholds quarrels, and the other raises doubts."

These days, in the United States, many politicians are lawyers, and some conservative evangelistic "Christians" and Christians want to influence politicians.

Factionalism is often found in politics: Republicans versus Democrats, conservatives versus liberals, idiots versus liberal Democrats. It is also found in religion: Protestants versus Catholics, Catholics and Protestants versus Muslims, Orthodox Jews versus Reformed Jews.

The second virgin continued:

"But good statesmen are bred in courts, camps, and cities; and they are not bred in schools and closets, at bars, and in pulpits."

This kind of camp is a military camp.

A closet is a private chamber.

The bars serve alcohol.

Hmm. Good statesmen are not bred in schools? Apparently, the schools Margaret Cavendish was referring to encouraged the reflective life and not the active life.

Most Prime Ministers of the United Kingdom since 1937 have studied at Oxford University.

The second virgin continued:

"And women are bred in courts and cities; they only lack the camp to give them the perfect state-breeding."

Again, this kind of camp is a military camp.

"Certainly, if we had that breeding, and did govern, we would govern the world better than it is," the third virgin said.

"Yes, because it cannot be governed worse than it is because the whole world is together by the ears, all up in wars and blood, which shows there is a general defect in the rulers and governors thereof," the fourth virgin said.

"Indeed the state counselors in this age have more formality and more ceremony than policy, and princes have more plausible words than rewardable deeds, insomuch as they are like fiddlers who play artificially and skillfully, yet it is just a sound that they make and give, and not real presences," the first virgin said.

State counselors in any age often look the part better than they live the part. Some fiddlers can play the notes in the right order but without any feeling, and some imitation blues singers can sing the words in the right order but without any blues.

The second virgin said:

"You say true; and as there is no prince who has had the like good fortune as Alexander the Great and Julius Caesar, so none have had the like generosities as they had, which seems to show that Lady Fortune (when she dealt in good earnest, and not in mockery) measured her gifts by the largeness of the heart, and the liberality of the hand of those she gave to."

When Julius Caesar died, he left his gardens to the city of Rome to be made a public park, and he left money for each Roman citizen.

Alexander the Great was generous in rewarding soldiers who distinguished themselves in battle.

The second virgin continued:

"And as for the deaths of those two worthies, she had no hand in them, nor was she in any way guilty thereof; for the gods distribute life and death without the help of Lady Fortune."

Julius Caesar died by assassination on the Ides of March of 44 B.C.E. His last words, said to his friend Brutus, who was one of the assassins, were "*Et tu, Brute?*" — "You, too, Brutus?"

Alexander the Great died from illness, most likely typhoid fever or malaria, in 323 B.C.E. His last words may have been these: "To the strongest." After his death, his four generals fought for control of his empire. They ended up dividing rulership of the lands he had conquered. The general named Ptolemy became Ptolemy I of Egypt. Cleopatra VII, a lover of Julius Caesar, was Macedonian, not Egyptian. When she died in 30 B.C.E., the Ptolemaic dynasty ended.

A matron said:

"It is strange, ladies, to hear how you talk without knowledge. Neither is it fit for such young ladies as you are to talk of state matters. Leave this discourse to the autumnal-year-olds of your sex, or old court-ladies who take upon themselves to know everything, although they understand nothing.

"But your discourses should be about masques, plays, and balls, and such like recreations fit for your youth and beauties."

Often, the young wish to rise, and the old wish to keep the young from rising.

— 2.4 —

Monsieur Malateste and Madame Bonit talked together.

"What's the reason you turn away Nan?" Monsieur Malateste asked.

"Why, she turns away me, for she is more willing to be gone than I to have her go," Madame Bonit answered.

"It is a strange humor — a strange mood — in you that you will never be pleased, for you are always quarreling with your servants," Monsieur Malateste said.

"Truly, I do not remember that I ever had a dispute or quarrel with any servant since I was your wife, before this with your maid Nan," Madame Bonit said. "And some evidence that what I say is true is that I do not speak many words in a whole day."

"Those words that you do speak, it seems, are sharp," Monsieur Malateste said.

"Let it be as you say, for I will not contradict you," Madame Bonit said.

"Well, then, take notice," Monsieur Malateste said. "I will not have Nan turned away."

"I am glad that she pleases you so well, and I am sorry that I can please you no better," Madame Bonit said.

— 2.5 —

Alone, Monsieur Frere said to himself, "She is very beautiful, extremely beautiful, beautiful beyond all the women whom nature ever made. O, I wish that she were not my sister!"

His sister, Madame Soeur, entered the room. He startled.

"I fear, brother, I have surprised you with my sudden coming in, for you startled," Madame Soeur said.

"Your beauty, sister, will not only surprise but also astonish any man who looks on it," Monsieur Frere said.

"You have accustomed yourself so much to dissembling courtships since you went into Italy that you cannot stop using them when talking to your sister," Madame Soeur said. "But please stop using that unnecessary civility when talking to me, and let us talk familiarly, as brothers and sisters are accustomed to do."

"With all my heart, as familiarly as you please," Monsieur Frere said.

"Please, brother, tell me if the women in Italy are beautiful, and what fashions they have, and how they are behaved," Madame Soeur requested.

Monsieur Frere said:

"To tell you in short, they are so artified — artificially made up — that a man cannot tell whether they are naturally beautiful or not.

"As for their behavior, they are very modest, grave, and ceremonious — in public and in private — confident, kind, and free, after a humble and insinuating manner. They are educated in all virtuosa — all the female arts — and especially they are taught to dance, sing, and play on musical instruments.

"They are naturally crafty, deceitful, false, covetous, "They are naturally crafty, deceitful, false, covetous, luxurious, and amorous; they love their pleasures better than Heaven."

According to the *Oxford English Dictionary*, "luxurious" means "Lascivious, lecherous, unchaste."

"As for their fashion of garments, they change as most nations do. As in most countries, their styles of garment go in and out of fashion. One fashion is supplanted by another.

"As for their houses, they are richly furnished, and they themselves are expensively adorned when they keep at home in their houses, for they dress themselves finest when they entertain strangers or acquaintances.

"But this relation of mine about Italian women is only about the courtesans.

"As for those who are kept honest, I can give little or no account, for they are so enclosed with locks and bolts, and they only look through a jealousy, so that a stranger cannot obtain a sight, much less an acquaintance."

The honest women of Italy look through only what their jealous husbands let them look through. At best they can look through small windows.

"Then they don't have that liberty we French women have?" Madame Soeur asked.

"O, no," Monsieur Frere answered.

"Why, do their Italian husbands fear that they would all turn courtesans if they should be left to themselves?" Madame Soeur asked.

"The men are jealous, and will not put it to the trial," her brother said, "for although they are all merchants, even the princes themselves, yet they will not venture their wives."

"Ventures" are risks, such as starting a new business.

In other words: Although these Italians are all businessmen and are accustomed to taking risks, yet they will not take the risk of allowing their wives freedom.

"I would not live there for all the world, for if I did I would be so restrained; for it is said that Italian men are as jealous of their wives as they are jealous of their brothers, fathers, and sons," Madame Soeur said.

According to Madame Soeur, Italian men are fiercely protective of their brothers, fathers, and sons as well as of their female family members.

The word "jealous," however, has many definitions in addition to "fiercely protective."

A cynical interpretation of her words would be she is saying that Italian men worry whether their brothers, fathers, and sons will make them cuckolds.

A cuckold is a man with an unfaithful wife.

An example of an unfaithful Italian wife is Francesca da Rimini in Canto 5 of Dante's *Inferno*. She slept with her husband's brother, he found out, and he killed them. Francisca and her brother-in-law, Paolo, are in the Inferno's second circle, which punishes the lustful.

"The Italian men are so, for they are wise, and they know that nature made all in common, and to a general use; for particular laws were made by men, not by nature," Monsieur Frere said.

A general use of living creatures is reproduction.

Human beings create particular laws, including laws about sex. Such laws, whether codified in a legal system or simply meant to be observed by custom in a society, can include Exodus 20:14: "*Thou shalt not commit adultery*" (King James Version). It can also include "Do not commit incest."

"They were made by the gods, brother," Madame Soeur said.

God created life. In doing so, He created sex.

"What gods, sister?" Monsieur Frere said. "Old men with long beards?"

"Bah, bah, brother, you are grown so wild in Italy that France, I fear, will hardly reclaim you; but I hope when you are married, you will be reformed and grow sober," his sister said.

"Why, sister, have you become more sober or reformed since you got married?" Monsieur Frere asked.

"No, brother," Madame Soeur said. "I never was wild or wanton, but always modest and honest."

"Indeed, sister, I think that you might have been married more to your advantage than you are, had not my father been so hasty in marrying you so young," Monsieur Frere said.

"Why do you say so, brother, when the man I'm married to is so worthy a person that I do not deserve him?" his sister said. "I would not change him for all the world."

"Sister, don't be angry; for it is my extreme love, having no more sisters but you, that makes me speak," Monsieur Frere said.

"Please, brother, do not think I am angry; for I believe it proceeds from love, and that it is your affection that makes you so ambitious for me," Madame Soeur said.

"Know, sister, I love you so well, and so much, that it is a torment to be out of your company," Monsieur Frere said.

"Thank you, brother, and know that I desire never to be in any other company than my husband, father, and brother; indeed, any other company is troublesome," Madame Soeur said.

According to Monsieur Frere, this is how chaste Italian women live.

Madame Soeur has said that Frenchwomen have freedom, but she is not using it.

— 2.6 —

The five sociable virgins and the two grave matrons met together.

"Ladies, how are your wits today?" a matron asked.

The word "wit" means intelligence. The word "wits" means the "faculty of reasoning and thinking in general," according to the *Oxford English Dictionary*.

The first virgin said: "Indeed, my brain is like Salisbury Plain today, where my thoughts run races, having nothing to hinder their way, and my brain, like Salisbury Plain, is so hard, that my thoughts, like the horse's heels, leave no print behind."

Salisbury Plain is a chalk plateau best known for being the site of Stonehenge and of the Westbury White Horse, a 180-foot image of a horse.

The first virgin continued:

"So therefore I have no wit today, for wit is the print, imprint, and mark of thoughts."

The first virgin mentioned races, which are contests that can be won — or lost. On this day, the virgins were complaining that they were finding it difficult to think well and to speak rationally.

"And I am sick today, and sickness breaks the strings of wit; and when the strings are broken, no harmony can be made," the second virgin said.

The third virgin said:

"It is with wits as it is with beauties; they have their good days, on which to speak quick and to look well, to look cloudy, and to speak dully."

Because the third virgin's wits were dull on this, a bad day, she left a few words (in bold below) out of her speech:

27

"It is with wits as it is with beauties; they have their good days, on which to speak quick and to look well, **and they have their bad days, on which** to look cloudy, and to speak dully."

The third virgin continued:

"And although my tongue today is apt to run like an alarm-clock, without any intermission, yet my mind being out of order, my tongue will go out of time, as either too fast or too slow, so that none can tell the true time of sense."

"For my part, I am so dull today that my wit is buried in stupidity, and I would not willingly speak unless my speech could work upon every passion in the heart, and every thought in the head," the fourth virgin said.

"For my part, if any people can take delight in my unfolded tongue and unpolished words, my discourse is at their service," the first virgin said.

"I think, ladies, your wits run nimbly, fly high, and spread far; and so therefore make a contest of wit, or a contest of eloquence," a matron said.

What is eloquent need not be rational.

Not all discourse needs to be rational. Flights of fancifulness can be nonrational and beautiful.

The nonrational lies between the rational (logic and math) and the irrational (sticking your hand in a blender and turning it on just to see what it feels like).

The realm of the nonrational is the realm of beauty, poetry, laughter, dance, sex, and love. Comedy is nonrational. The arts connect the world of the rational and the nonrational. Much intelligence goes into producing art, but much art explores the world of the nonrational.

Is it rational to create a 180-foot image of a horse on a chalk plain?

No, but it is a form of art and it is nonrational.

The first virgin responded, "With all my heart, for in the combat of eloquence I shall perform like a valiant man in a battle; for although he may not win the victory, yet he proves that he is not a coward. So, although I would not get the victory of wit or eloquence, yet I shall not prove that I am a fool."

The conversation turned to a criticism of speeches and of ancient historians.

Focusing on eloquence, and criticizing what her society considered eloquence to be, the second virgin said:

"I will make no such match, for, although I have read some few books, yet I have not studied logic or rhetoric to place and set words in order; and, although I have read history and such similar books, yet I have not got their speeches by heart, nor parts of them, as part of one oration and part of another oration, and parts of three or four other orations to make up an oration of my own, as all orators do nowadays.

"Neither have I studied the morals or the fathers so much as to have their sayings and sentences to stuff my discourse as preachers do, and to speak a natural way, although extraordinarily witty, as to have their orations as full of wit as of words, yet it would be condemned if the speaker were not learned, or if their speeches did not express learning."

The fathers are the patriarchs in the Old Testament, many of whom were poster boys of bad behavior but still ended up serving God. Look up the story of David, Bathsheba, and Uriah, the husband of Bathsheba.

This quotation has been attributed to many people: "To steal ideas from one person is plagiarism; to steal from many is research."

The third virgin said:

"Now that you talk about speeches and orations, it seems very strange to me to read the speeches that chronologers and historians write down to be truly related as from the mouths of those who spoke them, especially such as are spoken extempore and on a sudden, but more especially those that are spoken in mutinies and to a tumultuous multitude, wherein is nothing but distraction both in the speakers and hearers, frights and fears in opposers and assaulters.

"As, for example, when Tacitus set down the speeches of some persons at such times when and where everyone is in such fears and disorders as there seemed to be not any one person who could have the leisure, time, rest, or silence to get those speeches by heart, to bear them away in their memory, or had place, time, ink, pen, or paper to write them down."

True. Ancient historians do publish the "words" of other people although no one present would have been able to write down the speakers' actual words.

The fourth virgin said, "But the speeches that Thucydides sets down may be better credited because most of them were premeditated, and soberly, orderly, and quietly delivered, which might more easily be noted and exactly taken to deliver to posterity."

The third virgin said, "Another thing is how Tacitus could come to know the particulars and private speeches between man and man, as friend and friend, brother and brother. And not only the speeches of the Roman nations, of which he might be best informed, but the speeches of persons of other nations, whose language was not easily understood or frequent among the Romans. Nay, not only so, but he has written the thoughts of some commanders and others."

A matron said:

"Lady, you must not be so strict in history as to have every word true; for it is a good history if the sense, matter, manner, form, and actions are true."

In his *History of the Peloponnesian War*, Thucydides gave Pericles, the political leader of Athens, words in the Funeral Oration for a defense of democracy. The funeral oration by Pericles was not actually delivered in those exact words by Pericles: Thucydides wrote the funeral oration that appeared in his book. One purpose of the speech was to defend democracy, and the sense, matter, manner, form, and actions that Thucydides wrote were true to the historical Pericles.

Thucydides explained why he did this:

> As to the speeches which were made either before or during the war, it was hard for me, and for others who reported them to me, to recollect the exact words. I have therefore put into the mouth of each speaker the sentiments proper to the occasion, expressed as I thought he would be likely to express them, while at the same time I endeavoured, as nearly as I could, to give the general purport of what was actually said. (Translation by Benjamin Jowett)

The matron continued:

"For example, say that a man should be presented all naked. Is he less a man for being naked? Or is he more a man for being clothed, or for being clothed after another fashion than his own? So a history is not the less true if the actions, occasions, forms, and the like are related, although every word is not expressed as they were; so that Tacitus' speeches may be true, as to the sense, although he did express them after his manner, fancy, intelligence, or judgment. Thus the body or subject of those speeches might be true; only the dress is new."

Ancient historians such as Thucydides and Tacitus often wrote speeches and put them in the mouths of real people in their histories in order to illustrate important themes, including themes that were important to the "speakers" of the speeches.

For example, in Tacitus' *Annals of Imperial Rome*, the British female leader Boudicaa made an inspirational speech about freedom:

> *I am not fighting for my kingdom and wealth. I am fighting as an ordinary person for my lost freedom, my bruised body, and my outraged daughters. Nowadays Roman rapacity does not even spare our bodies. Old people are killed, virgins raped. But the gods will grant us the vengeance we deserve! The Roman division which dared to fight is annihilated. The others cower in their camps, or watch for a chance to escape. They will never face the din and roar of all our thousands, much less the shock of our onslaught. Consider how many of you are fighting — and why. Then you will win this battle, or perish. That is what I, a woman, plan to do! — let the men live in slavery if they will.* (Translation by Michael Grant.)

Ancient historians sometimes wrote competing orations. One oration would put forth one point of view. A second oration would follow and argue against that point of view. In doing this, ancient historians could provide competing views of a complex issue.

In the Mytilenean Debate in the third book of Thucydides' *History of the Peloponnesian War*, the Athenians decided to put the male citizens of Mytilene to death and to make the women and children of Mytilene slaves, and they sent a ship to Mytilene to carry out the orders. The next day, the Athenians, realizing the brutality of their decision, held a debate. Cleon made a speech in favor of the death sentence for all the male citizens of Mytilene, and Diodotus made a speech against the death sentence for all the male citizens of Mytilene. The debate resulted in their changing their mind. They sent a second ship after the first ship. The second ship arrived in time to prevent the original orders from being carried out.

Later in the war, the Athenians decided to put the male citizens of Melos to death and to make the women and children slaves unless the Melians submitted to them. In the Melian Debate, the Athenians stressed might: Their army was stronger and therefore the Melians ought to submit to them. The Melians, however, stressed justice. No agreement was made, the Melians fought and were conquered, and the Athenians killed all the men of Melos and made all the Melian women and children slaves.

The third virgin said:

"But with your permission, let me tell you that chronologers — historians — do not only new-dress truth but they also falsify her, as may be seen in our later chronologers: such writers as William Camden and the like. For they have written not only not impartially, but also falsely.

"As for particular families, some Camden has mistaken, and some of ancient descent he has not mentioned, and some he has falsely mentioned to their prejudice, and some so slightly — as with an undervaluing — as if they were not worth the mention, which is far worse than if he should rail or declaim against them.

"But I suppose he has done as I have heard a tale of a man who was a schoolmaster as Camden was, who went to whip one of his scholars, and the boy, to save himself, promised his master that if he would give him his pardon that his mother should give him a fat pig, whereupon the fury of the pedant was not only pacified but the boy was stroked [petted] and made much of.

"And so we can see that most schoolmasters commend scholars as being the most apt and ingenious in their learning, although those 'scholars' are mere dunces, because the dunces' parents and friends see or bribe the schoolmasters the most, which causes them both to flatter those 'scholars' and their parents.

"So Camden, to follow the practice of his profession, has sweetened his pen towards his scholars and their families, and it is likely sweetened most towards those scholars who were more beneficial to him. But to such persons whose parents had tutors for them at home, not allowing them to go to common schools, he has passed over or lightly mentioned their families, or has dipped his pen in vinegar and gall."

William Camden (1551–1623), headmaster of Westminster School, wrote *Britannia*, a historical survey of the British Isles, first published in 1586 and enlarged in later editions. In 1599, the herald Ralph Brooke published *A discoverie of certaine errours published in print in the much commended*

Britannia. In it, he complained about many genealogical and heraldic misrepresentations in the fourth edition of Camden's *Britannia*.

The first virgin said, "Indeed, it is likelier — quite likely — that he might take some pet — some offense — at those who did not entertain him at their houses when he went on his journey about the kingdom to educate himself about the several parts of the country, before he wrote about the same."

Camden's *Britannia* also included topographical information about Britain.

The second virgin said:

"I observed one error in his writing:

"That is, when he mentions such places and houses, he says, 'the ancient situation of such a worthy family,' when, to my knowledge, many of those families he mentions bought those houses and lands some one descent, some two descents, some three descents before, which families came out of other parts of the kingdom, or the city, and not to the ancient and hereditary families. But he leaves those ancient families unmentioned."

A "descent" is a generation.

In other words: Camden wrote about the newly rich families, but he did not give the old aristocratic families their due.

The fourth virgin said:

"Perhaps he thought it fitting that those families who were so ill husbands of their wealth or had so ill fortunes that they were forced to sell their ancient inheritance, should have their memories be buried in their ruins."

The fourth virgin then asked:

"What do you say about the chronologer of the gods and gallant heroes: Homer?"

Homer wrote the *Iliad* about an argument between Achilles and Agamemnon late in the Trojan War, and he wrote the *Odyssey* about Odysseus' travels and homecoming after the fall of Troy.

The Roman name for Odysseus is Ulysses.

"I say he was a better poet than a historian," the third virgin said.

"Why, Homer's works are only a poetical history, which is a romance; for romance writers heighten natural actions beyond natural power, as for example to describe by their wit impossible things yet to make them sound or seem probable," the second virgin said.

In Homer's *Iliad* old men such as Nestor can lift huge rocks that two men of today cannot lift.

"Nay, indeed, what is impossible can never be described as being probable," the first virgin said.

The fourth virgin said, "I am sure Homer was in the wrong — or else noble persons were not so well bred in his time as they are now in our time — as when he makes them miscall one another, giving one another ill names when they met to fight — such as 'dog' and the like names — when, in these our days, when noble persons meet to fight they bring compliments in their mouths and death in their hands, so that they compete as much in civility as courage. Indeed, true valor is civil."

Hector killed Achilles' best friend, Patroclus, during the Trojan War, and Achilles sought to avenge his death.

When Achilles and Hector met to fight each other to the death in Book 22 of the *Iliad*, Hector wanted to make an agreement that whoever killed the other would allow that person's corpse to be given to their family members so that it could be properly buried and the dead person's soul could enter the Land of the Dead.

In response, Achilles frowned and said, "No, Hector! You and I shall make no agreements. Do lions and men make agreements? Do wolves and lambs make agreements? No, the only thing that they have in common is that they hate each other. The same is true of you and me. We have no love for each other. The only thing we desire for the other is death. But let's fight. Use whatever courage you have, but it won't do you any good. You do not have long to live. You will pay for the grief you have caused me."

The first virgin said, "If you condemn Homer for making men to speak so, you may condemn him much more for making the gods to speak after that manner; for he has made the gods to speak so, as for example to call one another 'dogs' and the like names."

In Book 5 of the *Iliad*, Ares, god of war, fought the mortal Greek warrior Diomedes and was wounded. Ares fled to Mount Olympics, home of the most important Greek gods, and he complained about being wounded.

In response, Zeus said to Ares, "You are a whiner. Stop it. You are the god of war, and I hate you more than I hate any other of the Olympian gods. You love war, and you love battles, and you love suffering. You have the same kind of anger that your mother, Hera, has. But I do not want you to suffer. After all, you are my son. If you were not, I would have sentenced you long ago to dwell in the Land of the Dead."

The second virgin said:

"The truth is, Homer — as excellent a poet as he is famed to be — yet he has not fitted his terms of language proper to those he makes to speak, nor does he fit the behavior of those persons he presents proper to their dignities and qualities.

"For, as you say, he makes the gods in their contentions and fights not only to speak like mortals, but like rude-bred, ill-natured clowns, and to behave themselves like rude, barbarous, brutish, and cruel men, when he should have made the gods speak the most eloquent of humane language, and after the most elegant manner, the reason being that eloquence has a divine attraction, and elegance a divine grace.

Yes, Homer often makes the gods appear like clowns in the *Iliad*.

In Plato's *Republic*, Socrates argues that poets such as Homer ought to be banned because they incorrectly portray the gods.

In Book 14 of the *Iliad*, Hera, the wife of Zeus, king of the gods, seduces him so that he will go to sleep. This will allow the Trojans, whom Hera supports in the war, to rally in a battle that they are badly losing.

The Roman names of Zeus and Hera are Jupiter and Juno.

Zeus wants to sleep with his wife and he compliments her, but his way of complimenting her is to tell her that he desires her more than any other goddess or mortal woman he has slept with, and he reels off a long string of names.

Hera is a jealous wife, and this speech by her husband would make her NOT have sex with him except that she wants him to go to sleep so the Trojans can rally in the battle.

In Book 21 of the *Iliad*, the gods and goddesses fight a comic battle — not male versus female, but supporters of the Greeks versus supporters of the Trojans. On the human battlefield, warriors are fighting and dying, but the gods and goddesses are immortal and so cannot die. We can ask whether the gods and goddesses are capable of bravery if they are immortal.

Can gods and goddesses be heroes? Not if a hero is a person who risks his or her life for another person.

The second virgin wanted Homer to write romances, but Homer wrote epic poems.

"For my part, I can never read Homer upon a full stomach because if I do, I am sick to hear him describe their broiled, roast, and boiled meats," the third virgin said.

The first virgin said, "For my part I can read him at no time because my stomach is always so weak, or at least fussy, as the discourse of the large thighs or chines [the meat along the backbone] of beef and mutton, with their larded fat, suffocates my spirits and makes me ready to faint. For the discourse makes me imagine I smell the strong savor of the gross meats and the drunken savor of wine."

One reward for being a great warrior is getting the best food and the best wine.

"They had meat fit for soldiers, and not ladies," a matron said. "I hope their concubines who lay in their tents had finer meats, or else they would appear foul pursy — fat — sluts."

The word "slut" can mean a slovenly woman.

"Why, if they were, they would be handsome enough to serve those slovenly heroes," the fourth virgin said.

"Why do you call those great and brave heroes slovenly?" a matron asked.

"Because they killed and dressed — prepared for cooking — their own meat, and there are no such greasy fellows as butchers and cooks, and therefore they must necessarily stink most horribly," the fourth virgin said.

"It was a sign they had excellent stomachs in Homer's days," the second virgin said.

"That Homer could talk so often and long about meat was a sign that Homer had a good hungry stomach himself," the third virgin said.

In Homer's *Odyssey*, near the end of Book 8, a blind epic poet named Demodocus sings about the Trojan War. Odysseus, whose identity is not yet known to his hosts, rewards him with a savory cut of meat: the chine. In real life, a bard would have sung the *Odyssey* over three days. Possibly, the end of the first day's performance would have occurred soon after this event — and before Odysseus' telling about his Great Wanderings the next day. It is as if the singer of the *Odyssey* is subtly hinting for a tip from his audience.

"Let me tell you, ladies, it was a sign that those persons in those times were hospitable and noble entertainers of guests," a matron said, "but in these times the nobler sort are too curious — that is, too difficult to satisfy — and delicate."

The first virgin changed the topic: "I have observed that one pen may blot and blur a reputation, but one pen will hardly glorify a reputation."

"No; because to glorify requires many pens and witnesses, and even all that is little enough," the second virgin said.

The fourth virgin said:

"It is neither here nor there for that. For merit will get truth to speak for her in Fame's palace, and those who have no merit can never get in, or at least can never remain there. For haven't some writers spoken well of Nero and have striven to have glorified him, who was the wickedest of all the emperors?

"And haven't some writers done the like for Claudius, who was the foolishest of all the emperors? Yet they were never the more esteemed in the house of Fame.

"And haven't some writers written ill about and have endeavored to blot and blur the renowned reputations of Julius Caesar, Augustus Caesar, and of Alexander the Great?"

Certainly, a famous person's reputation can change for the better or for the worse over the centuries.

Over the last century, Emperor Claudius' reputation has much improved. Claudius' "Letter to the Alexandrian Embassy" affirmed Jewish rights in Alexandria and called for peace between Greeks and Jews. First published in 1924, the letter led to a reconsideration of Claudius' character.

The fourth virgin continued:

"And yet they are never the worse esteemed in the house of Fame. But heroic actions and wise governors force pens, although pens cannot force swords."

Heroic actions and wise governors inspire writers to write good things about them.

The second virgin said, "With your permission, let me say that pens and prints — printed publications— force swords sometimes, nay, for the most part; for don't books of controversies or engravings or printed laws make enemies, and such enemies as to pursue with fire and sword to death?"

Book burnings exist. Sometimes the opponents of books have burned more than books.

On 17 February 1600, Giordano Bruno was burned at the stake (with his tongue imprisoned in a vise of wood because of his beliefs) after the Roman Inquisition found him guilty of heresy. He wrote extensively, supported Copernicanism, and believed that the number of worlds is infinite. Today, he is a symbol of free speech and free thought.

The third virgin said, "Well, for my part, I don't believe that it was the glory of victory and conquering the most part of the world that made Alexander the Great and Julius Caesar to be so much reverenced, admired, and renowned by those following ages, but that their heroic actions were seconded by their generous deeds, distributing their good fortune to the most deserving and meritorious persons in their parties."

"You say the truth," the first virgin said, "and as there have been none so heroical since their deaths, so there have been none so generous."

"Ladies, excuse me, but you are unlearned, otherwise you would find that there have been princes since their times as heroical and generous as they were," a matron said.

"No, no. There have been none who had as noble souls as they had; for princes since their days have been ruled, checked, and awed by their petty favorites," the second virgin said. "Witness many of the Roman emperors, and others, when they ruled and checked all the world."

Suetonius' *The Twelve Caesars* is filled with salacious stories about Roman Emperors. Some earlier translations left the most salacious stories in Latin and put them in an appendix although the rest of the book was translated into English.

Many stories showing the Roman Emperors as evil people, however, are political propaganda by their enemies. According to Thorsten Opper, a curator in the Greek and Roman division of the British Museum, "Anything you think you know about Nero is based on manipulation and lies that are two thousand years old."

Tacitus accused Nero of being ruled by his mother, Agrippina, early in his Emperorship. He accused Nero of letting his mother rule him, and he accused mother and son of incest.

The fourth virgin said, "Indeed, princes are not so severe, nor do they carry that state and majesty as those in former times, for they neglect that ceremony nowadays, which ceremony creates majesty and gives them a divine splendor. For the truth is that ceremony makes them like gods, when the lack thereof makes them appear as ordinary men."

"Lack of ceremony necessarily makes them appear like ordinary men," the first virgin said, "for when princes throw off ceremony, they throw off royalty; for ceremony makes a king like a god."

"Then if I were a king or had a royal power, I would create such ceremonies that I would be deified, and so I would be worshipped, adored, and prayed to while I lived," the second virgin said.

"So would I, rather than to be sainted or prayed to when I were dead," the first virgin said.

"Why, ceremony will make you like a god both alive and dead, when without ceremony you will not be so much as sainted," the fourth virgin said.

"I prefer to be a saint than a god, for I shall have as many prayers offered to me as if I were made a god," the first virgin said.

Martin Luther (1483-1546) started the Protestant Reformation in the previous century. He was ordained as a priest in 1507.

The sociable virgins were talking as if they were Catholics.

A matron said, "Come, come, ladies, you talk like young ladies: You don't know what you are talking about."

In 2.3 the first virgin had said, "Indeed the state counselors in this age have more formality and more ceremony than policy, and princes have more plausible words than rewardable deeds, insomuch as they are like fiddlers who play artificially and skillfully, yet it is just a sound that they make and give, and not real presences."

Deeds are important, and ceremony can be important.

— 2.7 —

Madame Bonit and her maid, Joan, talked together.

Joan said, "Lord, madam, I wonder at your patience that you can let Nan not only be in the house and let my master lie with her — for she is more in my master's chamber than in yours — but to let her triumph and domineer, to command all as chief mistress, not only the servants, but yourself, as you have come to be under her command."

"Mistress" can mean 1) a female boss, and 2) a woman having an affair with a married man.

Madame Bonit's husband, Monsieur Malateste, was having an affair with the maid Nan, who bossed around everyone else, including Madame Bonit.

"How should I help it?" Madame Bonit asked. "What can I do about it?"

"Why, if it were up to me, I would ring my husband such a peal that would make him weary of his wench or of his life," Joan said.

She could complain so loudly that her husband would stop sleeping with the maid and would make him regret being alive.

Or she could ring (surround) her husband's penis with a peel (outer covering, aka vagina) in such a way that her husband would stop sleeping with the maid and would die (have an orgasm).

Actor Paul Newman once said about his wife, actress Joanne Woodward, "I don't like to discuss my marriage, but I will tell you something that may sound corny but that happens to be true. I have steak at home. Why should I go out for hamburger?"

Wedding rings are symbols. When a wedding ring is on a finger, both the wedding ring and the finger are symbols.

Think of John Belushi's samurai sword and scabbard.

The Latin word *vagina* means "sheath."

A sheath can be a scabbard: a container for a phallus-shaped object.

"Yes, so I may disquiet myself but not mend my husband; for men who love variety are not to be altered with either compliance or crossness," Madame Bonit said.

"That is true, if he would, or did, love variety; but he loves only Nan, a wench who has not the wit, nor the beauty, nor the good nature of your ladyship," Joan said.

"I thank you, Joan, for your commendations," Madame Bonit said.

"But many times a good-natured wife will make an ill-natured husband," Joan said.

"That's when men are fools and lack the wit and judgment to value worth and merit, or to understand it," Madame Bonit said.

"Why then, my master is one. But why will you be so good as to spoil your husband? For, in my conscience, I believe that if you were worse he would be better," Joan said.

"The reason is that self-love has the first place, and therefore I will not dishonor myself to mend or reform my husband," Madame Bonit said, "for everyone is to give account to Heaven and to the world of only their own actions, and not of any other's actions, unless it be as a witness."

"Then I perceive you will not turn away this wench," Joan said.

"It is not in my power," Madame Bonit replied.

"Try and see whether it is or not," Joan advised.

"No, I will not venture at it, lest I and my maid should be the public discourse of the town," Madame Bonit said.

"Why, if she should have the better, yet the town will pity you and condemn my master, and that will be some comfort," Joan said.

Even if Nan and Monsieur Malateste continued their affair, the sympathy of the town citizens would be for Madame Bonit.

"No, truly, for I had rather be buried in silent misery and be forgotten by mankind than live to be pitied," Madame Bonit said.

"Then I would, if I were you, make him a scorn to all the world by cuckolding him," Joan said.

"Heaven forbid that I should stain that which gave me a good reputation — my birth and family — or defame myself or trouble my conscience by turning into a whore for revenge," Madame Bonit said.

"Well, if you had seen what I have seen, you would hate him so much that you would study how to get a revenge," Joan said.

"What was that?" Madame Bonit asked. "What did you see?"

Joan replied, "Why, when you came into my master's chamber to see him when he was sick of the French pox, I think you chanced to taste of his broth that stood upon his table; and when you were gone, he commanded Nan to fling that broth out which you had tasted and to put fresh broth into the porringer to drink."

The French pox is venereal disease, especially syphilis. At this time, there were treatments but no cures for syphilis.

A porringer is a small bowl for porridge or broth.

Porridge is oatmeal or other meal boiled in water or milk.

"That's nothing, for many cannot endure to have their pottage blown upon," Madame Bonit replied.

Pottage can be porridge, soup, stew, or broth.

Joan said:

"It was not so with him.

"For before he drank the fresh broth, Nan blew it and blew it, and tasted it again and again to test the heat, and another time to test if it were salted enough, and he seemed to like it the better.

"Besides, he was never quiet while you were in the chamber, until you went out; he snapped at you at every word, and if you just touched anything that was in the chamber, he told you to leave it alone, and at last he told you to go to your own chamber and seemed well pleased when you were gone."

Madame Bonit said:

"Alas, those who are sick are always froward and peevish."

The word "froward" means "difficult to deal with."

She continued:

"But please, Joan, have more charity to judge for the best, and have less strong anger concerning my treatment."

CHAPTER 3

— 3.1 —

The five sociable virgins and the two grave matrons met together.

"Come, ladies, what will you discourse about today?" a matron asked.

"We will discourse about nature," the first virgin said.

"No, that is too vast a subject to be discoursed about because, the theme being infinite, your discourse will have no end," a matron said.

"You are mistaken; for nature lives in a quiet mind, feeds in a generous heart, dresses in a poetical head, and sleeps in a dull understanding," the second virgin said.

In other words, nature is not infinite because it is found within the individual.

"Nature's flowers are poets' fancies, and Nature's gardens are poetical heads," the third virgin said.

"Please, leave Nature in her garden and talk about something else," a matron said.

"Then let us talk about thoughts because thoughts are the children of the mind, begotten between the soul and the senses," the fourth virgin said.

"And thoughts are several companions, and, like courtly servitors, thoughts lead and usher the mind into several places," the first virgin said.

"Several" can mean 1) numerous, and 2) separate and distinct.

"Please, stop the discourse about thoughts because it's a dull discourse," the second virgin said.

"Then let us talk about reason," the fourth virgin said.

"Why should we talk about reason, when there are so many seeming reasons that the right cannot be known?" the third virgin asked.

"Seeming reasons" are apparent reasons. They may or may not be real reasons.

"Seeming reasons are like seducing flatterers who try to persuade people that all they say is truth, when all they say is false," the first virgin said.

"Let us talk about Justice," the second virgin said.

The fourth virgin said, "Justice, to the generality, has a broad full face; but to particulars she has only a quarter and half-quarter face, and to some particulars she veils it all over. Therefore, to talk about Justice is to talk with a blindfold on."

Punishment is given full force to most of the lower class (the poor), less strongly to most of the middle class, and not at all (or comparatively lightly) to most of the upper class (the rich).

To a multi-millionaire, a $100,000 fine may be a mild inconvenience. To a billionaire, it is at most a mild annoyance.

Justice should be blind, and to design a just society, the planners should not know ahead of time whether they will be lower class, middle class, or upper class.

Centuries later, John Rawls wrote about this in his *A Theory of Justice*, which was published in 1971. In deciding upon the rules for a just society, Rawls suggests that people ought to deliberate under a veil of ignorance; that is, people will not know in advance which position they will have in that society.

Therefore, in the original position (the position one is in before a society has been formed and before one knows one's position in it), one will not know one's economic status, one's race, one's creed, one's intelligence, one's career, etc.

Because of this, Rawls believes that people will form just rules. For example, if you don't know in advance what race you will be, you won't form Jim Crow rules because you may end up being the race that is discriminated against. If you don't know in advance whether you will be poor or wealthy, you won't make rules that favor the rich over the poor because you may be poor.

Rawls also believes that rational people will choose to obey the maximin rule, which states that we will choose the best of the worst situations (the "best-worse" outcome). In other words, we will choose a society that makes things as good as possible for the least advantaged citizens; after all, since we are behind a veil of ignorance, we don't know that we won't be among the least advantaged citizens: poor, with a low IQ and few skills, etc.

"Let us talk about bashfulness," the second virgin said.

"What! Should we talk about our own disgrace?" the third virgin said.

"A grace, you mean, lady," a matron said. "Bashfulness is a grace, not a disgrace."

"No, surely; a distempered countenance and a distorted face can be no grace," the third virgin said.

"Let us talk about the passions," the first virgin said.

Passions are strong emotions.

The second virgin said, "It is easier to talk about them than to conquer and govern them, although it is easier to conquer the perturbed passions of the mind than the unruly appetites of the body. For as the body is grosser than the soul, so the appetites are stronger than the passions."

By "appetites," the second virgin meant bodily desires, such as the desires for food, drink, and sex.

In Plato's *Phaedrus*, 253ff. appears the allegory of the chariot, which represents Humankind's tripartite soul. A charioteer drives a chariot drawn by two horses, which represent passions, aka desires. The white horse represents positive desires, such as the desire to achieve honor. The dark horse represents negative desires, such as the desire for drunkenness. The charioteer represents reason, which is needed to control the desires.

In Dante's *Inferno*, Circles 2 through 5 are devoted to the sins of incontinence. In Circle 2 are punished those who could not control their lust. In Circle 3 are punished those who could not control their desire for food and drink. In Circle 4 are punished the prodigal and the miserly: those who could not control their desire either for money or for the things that money can buy. In Circle 5 are punished those who could not control their anger.

Sins of incontinence occur when human beings do not use their reason to control their bad desires.

Sin also occurs when reason is misused. For example, much intellectual brain power can be used to support a heresy or to persuade people to do things that will endanger their soul or their body.

"Let us talk about gifts," the fourth virgin said.

"There are no gifts worth the talking about except natural gifts, such as beauty, wit, good nature, and the like," the fifth virgin said.

"Let us talk about wit," the fourth virgin said. "That is a natural gift."

The first virgin said:

"Nature gives true wit to very few, for many who are accounted wits are only wit-leeches that suck and swell with the wit of other men, and, when they are over-gorged, they spew it out again."

Good point, but author David Bruce once said, "Borrowed wit is better than no wit."

The first virgin continued:

"Besides, there are none except natural poets who have variety of discourses; all others talk according to their professions, practice, and studies, when poets talk of all that nature makes or art invents, and, similar to bees that gather the sweets of every flower, bring honey to the hive that are the ears of the hearers, wherein wit does swarm.

"But since we are not by nature so endowed, wit is a subject not fit to be pursued by us."

"Let us talk about beauty," the fifth virgin said.

"Those who have it take greater pleasure in the reputation of having it than in the actual possession of it because they don't care so much to talk about it as to hear the praises of it," the third virgin said.

"Come, ladies, let us go because I perceive that your wits can settle upon no one subject this day," a matron said.

They exited.

— 3.2 —

Monsieur Frere, alone and appearing to be melancholy, said to himself:

"O, how my spirit moves with a disordered haste!

"My thoughts tumultuously together throng, striving to pull down Reason from his throne and banish conscience from the soul."

He wanted to be incontinent and let his passion, not his reason, rule him.

He paced the floor with his arms folded.

In this culture, folded arms were a sign of melancholy. Unrequited lovers were melancholy.

His father, Monsieur Pere, entered the scene.

Seeing the folded arms, Monsieur Pere said, "What, Son, lover-like already, before you have seen your mistress? Well, her father and I are agreed; there's nothing lacking but the priest and ceremony, and all is done."

Monsieur Pere had arranged a marriage for his son, just as he had done for his daughter.

Monsieur Frere said, "Sir, there are our affections lacking because we have never seen one another, and therefore it is not known whether we shall feel affection and love for each other or not."

"I hope you are not so disobedient to dispute your father's will," Monsieur Pere said.

His dutiful daughter had not objected to the marriage that he had arranged for her.

"And I hope, sir, that you will not be so unkind as to force me to marry one whom I cannot love," Monsieur Frere said.

"Not love?" Monsieur Pere said. "Why, she is the richest heiress in the kingdom!"

Arranged marriages were often made to acquire wealth and social status. Such was the case here. They need not be love matches.

"I am not covetous for wealth, sir," Monsieur Frere said. "I had rather please my fancy than increase my estate."

"Your fancy?" Monsieur Pere said. "Let me tell you that your fancy is a fool, and if you do not obey my will, I will disinherit you."

"I don't fear poverty," Monsieur Frere said.

"Nor do you fear a father's curse?" Monsieur Pere asked.

"Yes, sir; that I do," Monsieur Frere replied.

"Why then, be sure you shall have my curse if you refuse to marry the woman I have chosen for you," Monsieur Pere said.

"Please, give me some time to consider it," Monsieur Frere said.

"Please do, and you had best consider wisely," Monsieur Pere said.

— 3.3 —

Two servants talked together about Madame Bonit.

"I fear that my lady will die," the first servant said.

"I fear so because the doctor, when he felt her pulse, shook his head, which was an ill sign," the second servant said.

"It is a high fever she is in," the first servant said.

"The doctor says a high continual fever," the second servant said.

"She's a fine young lady; it's a pity if she would die," the first servant said.

"My master puts on a sad face, but I think that his sadness does not appear to be that of a through-dye," the second servant said.

Monsieur Malateste's sadness was only on the surface; it was not deeply dyed into his soul.

— 3.4 —

The five sociable virgins and the two grave matrons met together.

"Come, ladies, how will you pass your time today?" a matron asked.

"Please let us sit and rhyme, and those who are out — at a loss and out of words — shall lose a collation — lose the competition — to the rest of the society," the first virgin said.

"Agreed, agreed," all the virgins and both the matrons said.

Their rhymes were about things that do not — or seem not to — go together: antithesis.

The first virgin rhymed:

"Love is both kind and cruel,

"As fire is to fuel;

"It does embrace and burn,

"Gives life, and proves death's urn."

Many weddings include the vow that the marriage will last "until death do us part."

But also, in this society, a "death" could be an orgasm.

An urn is a hollow, rounded vessel for containing something, or in this case, some thing.

A "thing" can be a penis.

"Proves" can mean "tests." Love can test death: Can love survive after death, perhaps in Paradise? Is death able to stop love?

The second virgin rhymed:

"A low'ring [rain-threatening] sky and sunny rays,

"Is like a commendation with dispraise;

"Or like to cypress bound to bays,

"Or like to tears on wedding days."

Laurel (bay) wreathes were worn as celebratory honors, while cypress sprigs were associated with funerals as a symbol of mourning.

Tears of sadness ought not to be shed on wedding days.

The third virgin rhymed:

"A flatt'ring tongue and a false heart,

"A kind embrace which makes me start [startles me],

"A beauteous form, a soul that's evil,

"Is like an angel, but [is] a devil."

The fourth virgin rhymed:

"A woman old to have an amorous passion,

"A Puritan in a fantastic fashion,

"A formal statesman who dances and skips about,

"And a bold fellow who is of countenance out."

A man who is out of countenance is abashed or disconcerted.

The fifth virgin rhymed:

"A scholar's head with old dead authors full,

"For want [lack] of wit is made a very gull [a complete fool]."

The fifth virgin spoke very little in the sociable virgins' discussions.

The first virgin rhymed:

"To laugh and cry, to mingle smiles and tears,

"Is like [similar] to hopes and doubts, and joys and fears;

"As sev'ral passions mixes in one mind,

"So sev'ral postures [expressions] in one face may find."

The second virgin rhymed:

"To love and hate both at one time,

"And in one person both to join,

"To love the man, but hate the crime,

"Is like to sugar put to [put in] brine."

"Crime" can mean "sin."

"Ladies, you had better tell some tales to pass your time with, for your rhymes are not full of wit enough to be delightfully sociable," a matron said.

"Agreed," the third virgin said. "Let us tell some tales."

The fourth virgin said, "Once upon a time Honor made love to Virtue. A gallant and heroic lord he was, and she was a sweet, modest, and beautiful lady, and naked Truth was the confidant to them both, which carried and brought love messages and presents from and to each other."

At this time, the phrase "made love to" meant "flirted with."

The second matron objected:

"Curses upon beastly Truth, for if she goes about naked, I dare say that she is a wanton wench.

"And Virtue, I dare swear, is little better than Truth herself if she keeps Truth's company or can behold her without closing her eyes.

"And I shall shrewdly suspect you, ladies, to be like her, if you talk about her; but even more, if you have any acquaintance with her.

"And, since you are so wild and wanton as to talk about naked Truth, I will leave you to your scurrilous discourse because I am ashamed to be in your company and to hear you speak such ribaldry.

"O, bah, O, bah, naked Truth! Jove bless me and keep me away from naked Truth, and also away from her sly companion, Virtue. Curses upon them both!"

The second matron exited and the sociable virgins followed her, saying "Stop, or else Truth will meet you and clothe you in a fool's coat."

The first matron followed them.

— 3.5 —

Madame Soeur and Monsieur Frere talked about the woman whom Monsieur Frere was supposed to marry.

"Now that you have seen your mistress, brother, tell me how you like her," Madame Soeur requested.

"Mistress" means "betrothed" here.

"It would be a rudeness to your sex if I should say I dislike any woman," Monsieur Frere replied.

"Surely, brother, you cannot dislike her; for she is beautiful, well-behaved, and well-bred, has a great estate and a good reputation, and is from a good family," Madame Soeur said.

"And may she have a husband who is suitable for and befitting her," Monsieur Frere replied.

"Why, she will have a suitable husband when she marries you," Madame Soeur said.

"I cannot equal her virtues or merit her beauty, so therefore I will not injure her with marriage," Monsieur Frere said.

"Won't you marry her?" Madame Soeur asked.

"No," Monsieur Frere said.

"I hope you are not speaking in earnest," Madame Soeur said.

"I am speaking the truth, sister," Monsieur Frere said. "I do not jest."

"Please, brother, do not tell my father that," Madame Soeur said. "For, if you do, he will be in such a fury that there will be no pacifying him."

"If you desire it, I will not," Monsieur Frere said.

"First reason with yourself and see if you can persuade your affections," Madame Soeur said. "See if you can love her."

"Affections, sister, can neither be persuaded either from or to," Monsieur Frere said. "For, if they could, I would employ all the rhetoric I have to persuade them. O, sister!"

He exited in a melancholy posture: His arms were folded.

Monsieur Pere entered the room and asked Madame Soeur, "Where is your brother?"

"He has just now gone away from here," Madame Soeur said.

"Why is it that he has not gone to his mistress?" Monsieur Pere asked.

The mistress was the woman he was supposed to marry and to love.

"I don't know, sir, but he looks as if he were not very well," Madame Soeur said.

"Not well?" Monsieur Pere said. "He's a foolish young man, and one who has had his liberty so much that he hates to be tied in wedlock's bonds. But I will go rattle him."

He was going to — perhaps metaphorically — slap some sense into his son.

"Please, sir, persuade him by degrees, and don't be too violent at first with him," Madame Soeur said.

"By the Mass, girl, thou give me good counsel, and I will persuade him gently," Monsieur Pere said.

— 3.6 —

Two or three maid-servants talked about the death of Madame Bonit.

"O, she's dead! She's dead!" the first servant said. "She was the sweetest lady in the world."

"O, she was a sweet-natured creature," the second servant said. "For she would never speak to any of us all — although we were her own servants — except with the greatest civility, as 'please do such a thing,' or 'call such a one,' or 'give or fetch me such or such a thing,' and all her servants loved her so well that they would have laid down their lives for her sake, unless her maid, Nan, were an exception."

"Well, I say no more," the first servant said, "but I pray to God that Nan has not given her a Spanish fig!"

In this context, a Spanish fig is a poisoned fig.

"Why, if she did, there is none of us who knows as much as we who can come as witnesses against her," the second servant said.

Nan entered the room and said, "It is a strange negligence that you stand prating here and do not go to help to lay my lady forth."

In this society, people came face to face with death. Instead of the corpse being cleaned and prepared in a hospital or funeral home, people did that in their homes.

Nan, the maid, exited.

Through the door, Monsieur Malateste could briefly be seen with his handkerchief before his eyes.

"My master weeps," the first servant said. "I did not think he had loved my lady so well."

"Pish, that's nothing," the second servant said, "for most people love the dead better than the living, and many will hate a friend when they are living and love them when they are dead."

— 3.7 —

Alone, Monsieur Frere stood in a room. He was crying.

Madame Soeur entered the room and asked, "Brother, why do you weep?"

"O, sister, mortality spouts tears through my eyes to quench love's raging fire that's in my heart! But it will not do; the more I strive, the more it burns with greater fury," Monsieur Frere said.

"Dear brother, if you are in love, she must be a cruel woman who will reject you because pure and virtuous love softens the hardest hearts and melts them into pity," Madame Soeur said.

"I wish that I were turned to stone and made a marble tomb, wherein lies nothing but cold death, rather than live tormented like this," Monsieur Frere said.

He exited.

Alone, Madame Soeur said to herself, "May Heaven keep my fears from proving to be true."

— 3.8 —

Monsieur Sensible and Mademoiselle Amour, his daughter, talked together. Mademoiselle Amour was the woman whom Monsieur Frere was supposed to marry. This was a marriage that their fathers had arranged.

"Daughter, how do you like Monsieur Frere?" Monsieur Sensible asked.

"Sir, I like whatever you approve of," Mademoiselle Amour replied.

"But setting aside your dutiful answer to me, tell me how you affect him," Monsieur Sensible requested. "Do you love him?"

"If I must confess, sir, I never saw any man I could love but him," Mademoiselle Amour said.

"You have reason to say that," Monsieur Sensible said. "For he is a fine gentleman, and those marriages most commonly prove to be happy when children and parents agree."

"But sir, he doesn't appear to fancy me as much or as well as I fancy him," Mademoiselle Amour said.

"When you begin to have doubts, it's a sign, child, that thou are in love," Monsieur Sensible said.

"No, sir," Mademoiselle Amour said, "but, if I thought he could not love me, I would take off that affection I have placed on him while I can master it, lest it should grow so strong as to become masterless."

"Fear not, child," Monsieur Sensible said.

— 3.9 —

The five sociable virgins and the two grave matrons met together.

"It is said that Malateste is a widower," the first matron said.

"Why, then there is a husband for me," the first virgin said.

One of the purposes of gossip is to find out who could possibly become your partner.

"Why for you? He may choose any of us as soon as you, for anything you know," the second virgin said.

"I'm sure we are as beautiful as you," the third virgin said.

"And we have as great marriage portions," the fourth virgin said.

In 1.7, the fourth virgin had said that she would never marry. She had then contradicted herself and said that if she married, she would marry a man who was old in years.

Marriage portions are dowries.

"And we are as well-bred as you are," the fifth virgin said.

A person who is well-bred comes from a good family and is well brought up: courteous and educated.

"Well, I know he is allotted to my share," the first virgin said.

"Please don't argue about him," the second matron said, "for surely he will have none of you all, for it is said he shall marry his maid."

53

"Why, he is not so mad because although his maid served to vex and grieve his wife into her grave, and also to pass away idle hours with him, yet he will not marry her, I dare assure you," the first virgin said. "For those who are married must take such as they can get, having no liberty to choose, but when they are free from wedlock's bonds, they may have choice."

Dressed in mourning clothes, Monsieur Malateste entered the room.

"So, sir, you are welcome, for you can resolve a question that is in dispute among us," the first virgin said.

"What is it, lady?" Monsieur Malateste asked.

"The question is whether you will marry your maid or not," the first virgin said.

"No, surely I cannot forget myself, nor my dead wife, so much as to marry my maid," Monsieur Malateste replied.

A man who forgets himself marries below his social class.

"Indeed, that is some kindness in husbands that they will remember their wives when they are dead, although they forget them while they live," the first virgin said.

The first virgin had no filter for her words.

"A good wife cannot be forgotten, neither dead nor alive," Monsieur Malateste replied.

"With your permission, sir, a bad wife will remain longest in the memory of her husband, because she vexed him most," the first virgin said.

"In my conscience, lady, you will make a good wife," Monsieur Malateste said.

Certainly, the first virgin was different from his first wife.

His first wife was very mild. The first virgin is not at all mild.

"If you think so, you had best try," the first virgin said.

This is known as the direct approach. Neither the first virgin nor Monsieur Malateste were shy about bringing up marriage immediately after his first wife had died.

Before modern medicine developed, people accepted as a fact that they would know death. Often families were large in part because the parents realized that one or more of their children would not live to adulthood. And married couples often were broken apart when one of the couple died. Because this was so commonplace, the surviving partner would often remarry quickly.

Early American colonists suffered from high rates of infant mortality. Often, a family would keep giving their children the same Christian name until one child finally survived. In addition, women frequently died in childbirth. At some old cemeteries, the husband would be buried along with several of his wives and several of their children who had died as infants or in childhood.

Only a few months after his first wife had died, Methodist preacher Joshua Thomas (1776-1853), aka "the Parson of the Islands," who lived in Maryland, proposed marriage to a young woman. She asked, "Isn't this rather sudden?" He replied, "But I've had my eye on you for quite a while."

"Shall I be accepted, lady?" Monsieur Malateste asked the first virgin.

"I know no reason I should refuse, sir; for gossip says you have a great estate, and I see you are a handsome man," the first virgin said. "And as for your nature and disposition, let it be as bad as it can be, mine shall match it."

"My nature loves a free spirit," Monsieur Malateste said.

His first wife was not a free spirit.

"And mine loves no restraint," the first virgin said.

This quotation has been attributed to Maya Angelou: "When someone shows you who they are, believe them the first time."

Certainly, the first virgin had shown that she was outspoken.

Her words could be interpreted as jesting and raillery, but she could be telling the truth.

"Lady, for this time I shall kiss your hands, and, if you will give me permission, I shall visit you at your lodging," Monsieur Malateste said.

"You shall be welcome, sir," the first virgin said.

He kissed her hands and then exited.

"Ladies, didn't I tell you that I should have him?" the first virgin asked.

"Jesting and raillery do not always make up a match," the second virgin said.

"Well, well, ladies, God be with you, for I must go home and provide for my wedding," the first virgin said. "For I perceive it will be done on the sudden because widowers are more hasty to marry than bachelors, and widows than maidens."

"Wait, lady, you must first get the good will of your parents," the first matron said.

The first virgin replied:

"All parents' good will concerning marriage is gotten beforehand, without speaking.

"If the suitor is rich, and if he proves to be a good husband, parents brag to their acquaintance, saying how well they have matched their child, making their acquaintance believe it was their prudence and industry that made the match, when the young couple had agreed to marry even before their parents ever knew or guessed at such a match.

"But if the marriage proves to be unhappy, then the parents complain to their acquaintance and shake their heads, crying, 'It was their own doings,' saying their children were willful and would not be ruled, although the parents had forced them to marry by the use of threats and curses.

"O, the unjust partiality of self-love, even in parents, which will not allow right to their own branches!

"But I forget myself. Farewell, farewell."

"Invite us to your wedding!" all the other virgins said. "Invite us to your wedding!"

CHAPTER 4

— 4.1 —

Monsieur Frere followed Madame Soeur into a room.

"Why do you follow me, with sighs fetched deep and groans that seem to rend your heart in two?" Madame Soeur asked her brother.

"Don't be offended. Sisters should not be so unnatural as to be weary of a brother's company or angry at their grief, but rather strive to ease the sorrow of their hearts than load on more with their unkindness," Monsieur Frere replied.

"Heaven knows, brother, that if my life could ease your grief I willingly would yield it up to death," Madame Soeur said.

"O gods, O gods, you cruel gods, you command nature to give us appetites, and then starve us with your laws, and decree our ruin and our fall — you create us only to be tormented!" Monsieur Frere said.

He exited.

His sister was alone in the room.

She said to herself, "I don't dare to ask about his griefs and sorrows or search his heart, for fear that I should find that which I don't want to know."

— 4.2 —

Monsieur Malateste and the first virgin had gotten married. She was now Madame Malateste.

Monsieur Malateste's steward, who managed the estate and home, now had orders to give to the household servants.

Monsieur Malateste's steward said:

"My master and our new lady are coming home, so you must get the house very clean and fine.

"You, wardropian, must lay the best carpets on the table and set out the best chairs and stools, and in the chamber in which my master and lady must lie, you must set up the cross-stitch bed and hang up the new suit of hangings."

A wardropian is in charge of wardrobes and cloth items.

What this society called a carpet, we would call a tablecloth.

The steward continued:

"On the new hangings is depicted the story of Abraham and Sarah, and her maid Hagar."

57

This story is told in Genesis 16 and 21.

Sarah was old and she had not given birth to a son, so she allowed Abraham to have sex with her maid Hagar in the hopes that she would give birth to a son. Hagar got pregnant and gave birth to a son named Ishmael, but later Sarah also got pregnant and gave birth to a son named Isaac.

When Hagar was pregnant and Sarah was not, Hagar grew proud. This is Genesis 16:2-4 (King James Version):

2 And Sarai said unto Abram, Behold now, the Lord hath restrained me from bearing: I pray thee, go in unto my maid; it may be that I may obtain children by her. And Abram hearkened to the voice of Sarai.

3 And Sarai Abram's wife took Hagar her maid the Egyptian, after Abram had dwelt ten years in the land of Canaan, and gave her to her husband Abram to be his wife.

4 And he went in unto Hagar, and she conceived: and when she saw that she had conceived, her mistress was despised in her eyes.

Hagar grew proud, and in the Malateste household, the maid Nan had grown proud.

The steward continued:

"And you, pantler, must take care that the glasses are well washed and that the basin and ewer, voider, and plates are brightly scoured, and also the silver cistern and the silver flagons standing therein, and to take care that the tablecloths are smooth and the napkins finely folded and perfumed, and that the lemons, oranges, bread, salt, forks, knives, and glasses are set and placed after the newest mode."

A pantler is in charge of the pantry and tableware.

A voider is a receptacle for waste food.

The newest mode of setting the table included setting out forks, which this society was beginning to use.

Nan entered the room.

Seeing her, the steward said:

"O, Mistress Nan, you have anticipated me, for I was going to seek you out to let you know my master and our new lady will be here before night, and therefore you must see that the linen is fine and the sheets are well dried and warmed, and that there are in my lady's chamber all things necessary."

"Let her command one of her own maids, for I am not one of her servants," Nan said.

"Why, whose servant are you?" the steward asked.

"My master's, who hired me and pays me my wages," Nan said. "I never saw his new wife, nor she me."

"But all my master's servants are also my lady's servants," the steward said, "for man and wife don't divide their servants; they don't say, 'Those are mine, these are yours.'"

"Why, I'm sure in my other lady's time all the servants were my master's, and none were my lady's," Nan said, "for she didn't have the power to take or turn away anyone."

Madame Bonit did no hiring or firing.

"The more was the pity, for she was both virtuous and wise, besides beautiful and well-bred, rich and honorably born, and of a sweet disposition," the steward said. "But it is said that this lady — the new wife — has such a spirit that she will share in the rule and government of the household."

"Yes, yes, for a little time, as long as honey-month lasts," Nan said. "I dare to assure you that she shall not reign or rule any longer."

A honey-month is the honeymoon period following a wedding.

Nan exited.

The steward said to the household servants, "Come, my friends and fellow-servants, let's every one go about our several and different affairs."

— 4.3 —

Mademoiselle Soeur was sitting in her chamber.

Previously, Margaret Cavendish had called Monsieur Frere's sister "Madame," which is used for married women. The title "Mademoiselle" can be used for young unmarried French-speaking women or for a young Frenchwoman.

Events will show that Monsieur Frere does not want his sister to be married.

Monsieur Frere came over to her and, kneeling down, he wept.

"Dear brother, why do you kneel and weep to me?" Mademoiselle Soeur asked.

"My tears, like distressed petitioners, fall to the ground and at your feet crave mercy," Monsieur Frere said. "It is not life they ask but love that they would have."

"Why, so you have; for I vow to Heaven I love you better than ambitious men love power or those who are vainglorious love a reputation, better than the body loves health or the life loves peace," Mademoiselle Soeur said.

"Yet still you don't love me as I would have you love me," her brother said.

"Why, how would you have me love you?" Mademoiselle Soeur asked.

"As husbands love their wives, or wives love their husbands," her brother said.

"Why, so I do," Mademoiselle Soeur replied.

"And will you lie with me?" her brother asked.

He was asking his sister if she would have sex with him.

"What!" she exclaimed. "Would you have me commit incest?"

"Sister, don't follow those foolish binding laws that frozen men have made, but follow nature's laws, whose freedom gives a liberty to all," her brother said.

"Heaven bless your soul, for surely you are possessed with some strange, wicked spirit that is not accustomed to wander among men," Mademoiselle Soeur said.

Her brother said, "Sister, don't be deceived with empty words and vainer tales, made only at the first to keep the ignorant common sort of people in awe, whose faith, like their greedy appetites, take whatever is offered; they never consider whether it is bad or ill to their stomachs, but instead they think all is good that they can get down. So whatever they hear, they think it is true, although they have no reason or possibility for it."

"But learned and knowing men, wise and judicious men, holy and good men, know that what you ask for is wicked," Mademoiselle Soeur said.

"They do not know it, but they believe as they are taught; for what is taught men in their childhood grows strong in their manhood, and as they grow up in years, so they grow up in superstition. Thus wise men are deceived and cozened by length of time, taking an old forgotten deed to be a true sealed bond.

"Therefore, dear sister, your principles are false, and therefore your doctrine cannot be true," Monsieur Frere said.

"Heaven has taught that doctrine, and therefore we cannot err in obeying it," Mademoiselle Soeur said.

Leviticus 18:9 states, "*The nakedness of thy sister, the daughter of thy father, or daughter of thy mother, whether she be born at home, or born abroad, even their nakedness thou shalt not uncover*" (King James Version).

Deuteronomy 27:22 states, "*Cursed be he that lieth with his sister, the daughter of his father, or the daughter of his mother. And all the people shall say, Amen*" (King James Version).

One argument against incest is that offspring are more likely to be deformed. Google photos of the Hapsburg lip or Hapsburg jaw. Most of the marriages of the Spanish Hapsburgs in the 17th century were between close relatives, leading to inbreeding.

Another argument against incest is that incest can cause problems such as jealousy in the family.

A third argument against incest is that in cases involving children, the child is not of age to give consent.

"Heaven considers us no more than beasts that freely live together," her brother said.

A woman was astonished that her cat had kittens because her cat never went out of her apartment and was never around tomcats. A friend heard this story and pointed to a tomcat in the apartment and asked, "What about him?" The woman answered, "Oh, he's her brother."

"O, that I should live to know my only brother has turned from man to beast!" Mademoiselle Soeur said.

She exited.

Alone, Monsieur Frere said to himself, "I am glad that the ice has been broken and that her fury does not rage like fire."

— 4.4 —

Monsieur Sensible and Mademoiselle Amour talked together. Mademoiselle Amour was a young unmarried Frenchwoman.

Monsieur Sensible said, "Daughter, I perceive that Monsieur Frere neglects you. Besides, he is a wild, debauched young man, and in no way likely to make a good husband. Therefore, I charge you on my blessing and the duty you owe me to draw off those affections you have placed upon him."

"Good sir, do not impose on my duty that which I cannot obey," Mademoiselle Amour said. "For I can sooner draw the light from the sun, or the world from its center, or the fixed stars from their assigned places, than draw away love from him."

This society referred to planets as stars. The wandering stars are planets that move in the sky. The fixed stars do not move in relation to each other and make up the unchanging constellations and the Milky Way.

To "draw [...] the world from its center" may mean to "move the Earth from where it is now."

Using the Ptolemaic geometric model, the Earth is at the center of the universe; however, Copernicus (1473-1543) had developed the heliocentric model that placed the Sun at the center of the solar system and Galileo (1564-1642) had championed Copernicus' work. *The Unnatural Tragedy* was published in 1662.

"Why, what if he will not have you?" Monsieur Sensible asked.

"I can only say I shall be unhappy," Mademoiselle Amour replied.

"I hope you will be wiser than to make yourself miserable for one you cannot have to be your husband," Monsieur Sensible said.

— 4.5 —

Many of Monsieur Malateste's servants were waiting for their master and lady to enter their home. Madame Malateste was formerly the first virgin.

Monsieur Malateste and Madame Malateste arrived.

"May Heaven give your worship joy, and our noble lady," the servants said.

"What! Is this your best house?" Madame Malateste asked.

"Yes, and isn't it a good one, sweetheart?" Monsieur Malateste asked.

Madame Malateste said:

"Bah, I hate such an old-fashioned house, so therefore please pull it down and build another that is more fashionable, so that there may be a *bellevue* and pergolas around the outside of the house."

Pergolas are 1) raised balconies, and 2) covered walkways in a garden.

A *bellevue* is French for a beautiful view.

Madame Malateste was being unreasonable here. Tearing down the old house and building a new house would not change the view from the house. She was establishing dominance over her husband.

Madame Malateste continued:

"Also, arched gates, pillars and pilasters, and carved frontispieces with antic imagery."

Pilasters are rectangular columns that project from a wall.

A frontispiece in architecture is a decorative area above a main entrance.

"Antic imagery" is grotesque imagery.

Madame Malateste continued:

"Also, I would have all the lower rooms vaulted and the upper rooms flat-roofed, painted and gilded, and the planchers chequered and inlaid with silver."

Given that most roofs are designed not to be flat (so rain and melting snow would fall off), space would be wasted if the lower rooms were vaulted and the upper rooms were flat-roofed.

Planchers are floors or ceilings made from wooden planks.

Madame Malateste continued:

"The staircase is to be large and winding, the steps broad and low as shallow; then to take in two or three fields about your house to make large gardens in which you may plant groves of myrtle; as also to make walks of green turf, and those to be hanging and shelving as if they hung by geometry. Also, fountains and waterworks, and those waterworks to imitate those birds in winter that only sing in summer."

The steps of the staircase were to be broad and low and shallow; in other words, there were to be more stairs than were necessary, which would increase the expense of building the staircase.

She was asking for "walks of green turf." Normally, these would be on the ground and people would walk on them. But she wants them "to be hanging and shelving as if they hung by geometry." Think of the Hanging Gardens of Babylon. Now imagine that the Hanging Gardens include hanging walks.

An example of waterworks is a cascade: a small waterworks. If the cascades were "to imitate those birds in winter that only sing in summer," the waterfalls would be silent. Cascades are not silent, so Madame Malateste was again being unreasonable in order to assert dominance over her husband.

"But this will cost a great sum of money, wife," Monsieur Malateste objected.

Much of what Madame Malateste wanted such as carved frontispieces with antic imagery was decorative rather than necessary and it was expensive.

"That's true, husband, but for what use is money unless to spend?" Madame Malateste replied.

"But it ought to be spent prudently," Monsieur Malateste said.

"Prudently, do you say? Why, prudence and temperance are the executioners of pleasure and the murderers of delight, and therefore I hate them, just as I also hate this covetous humor of yours," Madame Malateste said.

Some people are covetous for money. Some people are tight-fisted.

Other people are spendthrifts.

Aristotle advocated a mean between the extremes of miserliness and wastefulness.

Monsieur Malateste and Madame Malateste exited.

"Aye, by the Virgin Mary, sir; here is a lady indeed," the first servant said. "For she talks of pulling down this house before she has thoroughly seen it, and of building up another."

"If you will have my opinion, the old servants must go down as well as the old house," the second servant said.

"I believe so," the third servant said, "for she looked very scornfully upon us, nor did she speak one word either good or bad to us.

"Well, let us go about our employments and please as long as we can, and when we can please no longer we must seek other employment," the fourth servant said.

The first virgin had shown intellectual ability in her discussions with the other sociable virgins. In a different kind of society, one that allowed women more freedom and ambition, Madame Malateste might be able to conquer more than her husband.

— 4.6 —

Monsieur Frere and Madame Soeur talked together.

"Do not pursue such horrid acts as to whore your sister, cuckold your brother-in-law, dishonor your father, and brand your life and memory with black infamy," Madame Soeur said. "Good brother, consider what a world of misery you strive to bring upon yourself and me."

"Dear sister, pity me, and let a brother's pleading move your heart, and don't bury my youth in death before the natural time," Monsieur Frere said.

"It is better you should die, and in the grave be laid, than live to damn your soul," Madame Soeur said.

"To kill myself will be as bad a crime," Monsieur Frere said.

In this society, sins were called crimes.

In Dante's *Inferno*, the suicides are punished in Circle 7, which punishes the violent. Suicide is violence against oneself. The Suicides are punished in a gloomy wood. The Suicides, in fact, are the grubby shrubs of the wood. They can communicate only when a twig or branch is broken, for then they use the resulting hole as a mouth until the blood congeals. This punishment is appropriate because by killing themselves, the Suicides gave up the privilege of self-determination. As shrubs, the Suicides have no free will because plants have no free will. This is appropriate because in life the Suicides rejected free will by committing suicide. As grubby shrubs, the Suicides cannot move around and cannot even speak unless someone breaks off a twig or branch. At the Last Judgment, the Suicides will be given back their bodies, but because they rejected their bodies when they were alive, the bodies will hang from the branches of the shrubs.

Rape is sexual violence, and those who are violent against other people are also punished in Circle 7.

Those who were treacherous against kin/family are punished in the first of four rings of the Ninth and Deepest Circle. The first ring, Caina, is named after Cain, who slew Abel. The sinners are frozen in ice up to their neck. The Ninth Circle is where the worst sinners are punished.

"O, no," Madame Soeur said. "For death in any way is more honorable than such a life as you would live."

Cato the Younger is also known as Cato the Stoic and as Cato of Utica. In his life, he was renowned for possessing Prudence, Temperance, Justice, and Courage in abundance. He was morally upright. He understood law. He valued freedom. He declined to take bribes. He detested the corruption of his age. When war broke out between Julius Caesar and Pompey the Great, Cato sided with Pompey because he believed that Julius Caesar was the greater enemy of freedom. When Julius Caesar decisively defeated Pompey at Utica, Cato committed suicide there rather than submit to a person whom he considered to be a foe of freedom. Cato was a suicide, a pagan, and an opponent to Julius Caesar, but he was virtuous.

Cato the Younger works on the lowest level of the Mountain of Purgatory, making sure that the saved souls keep their minds on purging their sins, not on frivolous matters. Some people think Cato is saved and will enter Paradise;

other people think that when Cato's job is done, he will go to the First Circle of the Inferno — Limbo — and be with the other virtuous pagans.

— 4.7 —

Two gentlemen talked together.

"Friend, please tell me why you do not marry," the first gentleman asked.

"Because I can find no woman who is exactly what I would have a wife to be," the second gentleman said. "For first, I would not have a very tall woman, for she appears as if her soul and body were mismatched, as if she would have a pigmy soul and a giant body."

"Perhaps her soul is answerable to her body," the first gentleman said. "Perhaps her soul is as big as her body."

The second gentleman said:

"O, no, for it is a question whether women have souls or not. But, for certain, if they have souls, their souls are of a dwarfish kind.

"Neither would I have a wife with a masculine strength, for it seems preposterous to the softness and tenderness of their sex."

Some men feel the same way today. Jenny Thompson won eight Olympic gold medals in swimming, a sport that requires strong arms. Once, a guy she was dating told her that although he liked her, her arms freaked him out. She worried briefly and then decided, "My arms are what make me swim so fast and they're part of who I am." She added, "Being a strong woman and an athlete isn't entirely acceptable in society."

The second gentleman continued:

"Neither would I have a lean wife, for she would appear always to me like the picture of Death, if she just had a scythe and hour-glass in her hand. For, although we are taught to always have death in our mind — to remember our end — yet I would not have Death always before my eyes, to be afraid of my end. But to have a very lean wife would be to have Death in my arms as much as in my eyes, and my bed would be as my grave."

Death is often portrayed as a skeleton, which is the leanest a body can be.

"Your bed would be a warm grave," the first gentleman said.

"Why, man, although death is cold, the grave is hot," the second gentleman said, "for the earth has heat, though death has none."

In this society, "earth" means "the action of plowing." Metaphorically, in bed, it can generate much heat.

In this society, "death" is an orgasm, following which heat dissipates.

Literally, the Earth does have heat. Its core is molten.

Literally, after death corpses rapidly cool.

"What do you say about a fat woman?" the first gentleman asked.

"I say a fat woman is a bedfellow only for the winter and not for the summer," the second gentleman said, "and I would want to have a woman for my wife who would be a nightly companion all the year."

"I hope you would not make your wife such a constant bedfellow that you would lie always together in one bed," the first gentleman said.

"Why not?" the second gentleman said.

"Because a man's stomach or belly may ache, which will make wind work, and the rumbling wind may decrease love, and so your wife may dislike you, and her dislike, in time, may make you a cuckold," the first gentleman said.

Wind, of course, is flatulence.

The second gentleman said:

"With your permission, let me say that it increases matrimonial love!

"It is true, it may decrease amorous love, and the more amorous love increases, the more danger a man is in. For amorous love even to husbands is dangerous, for that kind of love takes delight to progress about, when matrimonial love is constant and considers nature as it is.

"Besides, a good wife will not dislike that in her husband which she is subject to herself."

In answer to the question "How did you accidentally kill the mood during consensual sex?" that was posted on the AskWomen subReddit on Reddit.com, Justcameheretovote wrote, "[...] there was the time it was hot and we [she and her husband] were a bit sweaty. Our chests rubbed together and made a fart noise [...]. We were laughing so hard we couldn't recover. We're super mature."

The second gentleman continued:

"But, whatever happens, I will never marry unless I can get such a wife as is attended by virtue, directed by truth, instructed by age on honest grounds and honorable principles, which wife will neither dislike me, nor I her, but the more we are together the better we shall love, and live as a married pair ought to live, and not as dissembling — lying — lovers, as most married couples do."

John Custis and Fidelia Custis were not happy after they were married. Once, they attempted a reconciliation and even drew up a contract between each other. In the contract, they agreed, among other things, not to hide the other's silverware.

As part of the attempt at reconciliation, they took a carriage drive together along Chesapeake Bay. However, John grew angry when Fidelia stayed silent, and so he drove his team and carriage into the bay. This prompted Fidelia to ask, "Where are you going, Sir?" Her husband told her, "To hell, Ma'am." Fidelia replied, "Drive on, then."

When John Custis died, his tombstone stated that although he was 71 years old, he had lived only seven years — the years he had been an adult bachelor.

"What do you think of choosing a wife from among the sociable virgins?" the first gentleman asked.

The second gentleman said:

"No, no, I will choose none of them, for they are too full of discourse. For I would rather have a wife with a listening ear than a talking tongue, for by the ear she may receive wise instructions, and so learn to practice that which is noble and good; also to know my desires, so that she would obey my will, when by speaking much she may express herself a fool. For great talkers are not the wisest practitioners."

Of course, if what the second gentleman says is true, husbands would not be the wisest practitioners because they are the ones who do the talking.

The second gentleman continued:

"Besides, her restless tongue will disturb my contemplations, the tranquility of my mind, and the peace, quiet, and rest of my life."

Quite possibly, the husband's restless tongue would disturb the wife's peace, quiet, and rest of her life.

In this society, many people considered a good wife to be an obedient wife.

— 4.8 —

Madame Malateste, a maid, and Nan, the former lady's maid, were in a room together. The former lady, of course, was the late Madame Bonit.

"Are you she — the woman — who takes upon you to govern and to be mistress in this house?" Madame Malateste asked Nan.

"Why, I do, but that I did in the other lady's time," Nan said.

"Let me tell you, you shall not do so in my time," Madame Malateste said. "Nay, you shall have no doings in my house. Therefore, get out of the house."

"I will not go," Nan said.

"No?" Madame Malateste said. "But you shall."

She said to her other maid, "Go, and call one of those servants I brought with me."

This would be a servant who was loyal to her.

The maid exited, and a man-servant entered the room.

Madame Malateste said to him, "Here, take this wench and put her out of the gates."

Madame Malateste exited.

"You rogue!" Nan said to the man-servant. "Touch me if you dare — I shall have one to defend me."

"I defy your champion," the man-servant replied.

He picked her up and carried her. She shrieked.

Monsieur Malateste entered the room.

"What, you villain, will you force her?" he said to the man-servant. "Will you rape her? Set her down."

"I did no more than what I was commanded to do," the man-servant said.

"Who commanded you to do that?" Monsieur Malateste asked.

"My lady, sir, commanded me to carry her out of the gates," the man-servant replied.

"Please let her alone until I have spoken with my wife," Monsieur Malateste said.

"I shall, sir," the man-servant said.

He set Nan down.

The man-servant exited.

Nan cried.

"What's the matter, Nan?" Monsieur Malateste asked.

"Only my lady's dislikes of my person," Nan said, "for it could not be through any neglect of my service, or faithful diligence, or humble duty, but through a passionate humor, because she has heard you were pleased before to favor me."

"But now we are very honest, Nan," Monsieur Malateste said.

"Honest" means "chaste."

Now he was faithful to his wife.

"Yes, the more unkind man you, to win a young maiden to love and then to turn her away in disgrace," Nan said.

"To turn away" means "to fire" and "to send away."

"I do not turn you away," Monsieur Malateste said.

"Yes, you do, if you allow my lady to turn me away," Nan said.

"How should I help that?" Monsieur Malateste said. "For she has such a strong spirit that she cannot be controlled."

"O, sir, if you bridle her, you may guide her as you will," Nan said.

"How should I bridle her?" Monsieur Malateste asked.

"Why, put her to her allowance, and take the government of your family out of her hands, as you did to your former lady," Nan said.

This means to give her a small allowance and not allow her to control the household accounts, which have much money that she would control.

"My other wife was born with a quiet obedient nature, and this wife was born with a high and turbulent nature, and if I should cross her high working spirit she would grow mad," Monsieur Malateste said. "She would become insane."

"Why, then you would have a good excuse to tie her up," Nan said.

"Her friends would never allow me to do that," Monsieur Malateste said. "Besides, the world would condemn me and consider me a tyrant."

"Why, it is better to be considered a tyrant than a fool," Nan said.

"O, no!" Monsieur Malateste said. "For men ought to be sweet and gentle-natured to the effeminate sex."

Nan replied, "I see by you that the worse that men are treated, the better husbands they make; for you were both unkind and cruel to your other lady, neither could you find, or at least would not give, such arguments for her."

Monsieur Malateste had not been sweet and gentle-natured to his previous wife.

"Will you rebuke me for that which you persuaded me to do by dispraising and criticizing your lady to me?" Monsieur Malateste asked.

Nan replied, "Alas, sir, I was so fond of your company that I was jealous even of my lady, and love is to be pardoned. Therefore, dear sir, don't turn me away; for Heaven knows I desire to live no longer than when I can have your favor, and I wish I were blind if I might not be where I may see you, and my heart leaps for joy whenever I hear your voice. Therefore, good sir, for love's sake pity me."

Nan appeared to cry.

"Well, I will speak to my wife for you," Monsieur Malateste said.

He exited.

Alone, and not crying, Nan said to herself:

"Well, if I can get my master to 'dance' just once, to kiss me again — which I will be industrious in working to accomplish — I will be revenged on this domineering lady."

This kind of "dance" is done in bed.

Nan continued:

"I hope I shall be too crafty for her."

CHAPTER 5

Monsieur Frere and Mademoiselle Soeur talked together.

Mademoiselle Soeur said, "Brother, speak no more on so bad a subject, for fear I would wish you unable to speak because the very breath that's sent forth with your words will blister both my ears. I would willingly hide your faults — nay, I am ashamed to make them known — but if you persist, by Heaven I will reveal your wicked desires, both to my father and my husband."

"Will you do that?" Monsieur Frere asked.

"Yes, I will do that," Mademoiselle Soeur answered.

"Well, I will leave you and see if reason can conquer my evil desires, or else I'll die," Monsieur Frere said.

"May Heaven pour some holy balm into your festered soul," Mademoiselle Soeur said.

Monsieur Malateste and Madame Malateste, his wife, spoke together.

"Wife, I have come as a humble petitioner to you on the behalf of Nan," Monsieur Malateste said. "She has been a servant here ever since I was first married to my other wife."

"No, no, husband, I will have none of your whores in the house where I live," Madame Malateste said. "If you must have whores, go seek them abroad — out of this house."

"Please don't let your jealous passion turn away a good servant," Monsieur Malateste said.

"Would you rather please your servant — a whore — or me?" Madame Malateste asked.

"Why, you," Monsieur Malateste answered.

"Then turn her away," Madame Malateste said. "Fire her."

"But surely, wife, you will let me have enough power to keep an old servant," Monsieur Malateste said.

"No, husband," Madame Malateste said. "Not if your old servant is a young lusty wench."

Monsieur Malateste said, "But I have given my word that she shall stay."

Madame Malateste said, "And I have sworn an oath that she shall go away."

"But my promise must be kept, and therefore she shall not go away," Monsieur Malateste said.

"I say she shall go away," Madame Malateste said. "Nay, more, I will have her whipped at the end of a cart and then sent out of doors."

As a legal punishment, prostitutes used to be led around town at the end of a cart and whipped.

"As I am master, I will command no one shall touch her, and let me see who dares to touch her," Monsieur Malateste said.

"Who dares to touch her?" Madame Malateste said. "Why, I can hire poor fellows for money, not only to whip her but to murder you."

"Are you so free with my estate?" Monsieur Malateste said. "I will discharge you of that office of keeping my money."

An office is a job or a position with responsibility. His wife was responsible for controlling the household accounts.

"If you do, I have youth and beauty that will hire for me revengers and get me champions," Madame Malateste said.

"Will you do that?" Monsieur Malateste asked.

"Yes, or anything rather than not get what I want," Madame Malateste said. "And know that I perfectly hate you for taking my maid's part against me."

"Nay, please, wife, don't be so angry," Monsieur Malateste said, "for I said all this just to test thee."

"You shall prove me, husband, before I have done," Madame Malateste said.

She had been put to the test, and she would prove to be not like his former wife.

— 5.3 —

Alone, Madame Soeur said to herself:

"Shall I divulge my brother's crimes, which are such crimes as will set a mark of infamy upon my family and race forever?

"Or shall I let vice run without restraint?

"Or shall I prove false to my husband's bed, to save my brother's life?

"Or shall I damn my soul and my brother's soul, to satisfy his wild desires?

"O, no, we both will die to save our souls, and keep our honors clear."

Marks of infamy are stigma. Criminals at this time could be branded. Anyone seeing the brand would know that the person with the brand had been found guilty of a crime.

In the case of the family of Madame Soeur and Monsieur Frere, the mark of infamy would be metaphorical.

— 5.4 —

Alone, Monsieur Frere said to himself:

"The more I struggle with my affections, the weaker I grow to resist.

"If gods had power, they surely would give me strength, and if they were just, they would exact no more than I could pay; and if they cannot help, or will not help me, then, Furies, rise up from the infernal deep and give my actions aid."

The Furies are goddesses of vengeance. They especially punish those who murder family members. For example, Aeschylus' *Oresteia* is a trilogy of plays about the Furies pursuing Orestes after he murdered his mother, Clytemnestra, after she had murdered his father, Agamemnon, leader of the Greek forces against Troy.

Monsieur Frere continued:

"Devils, assist me, and I will teach you to be more evil than you are, and when my black and horrid designs and plans are fully finished and fully accomplished, then take my soul, which is the quintessence of wickedness, and squeeze some venom forth upon the world that may infect mankind with plagues of sins."

He would teach the devils to do more evil acts by example.

His soul's venom would poison Humankind and turn humans evil.

Monsieur Frere continued:

"There in the world multitudes will bury my sins, or multitudes will regard me as a saint and offer sacrifices at my shrine."

Either his sins would be buried by the multitudes of people committing multitudes of sins, or the now-evil people would offer sacrifices to him.

The now-evil people could regard him as a god of evil, and therefore a saint of evil.

Or they could regard him as a good saint because their sins would be so much more evil than his, so thoroughly would his soul's venom corrupt the humans.

Monsieur Malateste and his maid, Nan, talked together.

"Nan, you must be contented, for you must be gone," Monsieur Malateste said, "for your lady will not allow you to be in the house."

"Will you visit me if I should live near your house, at the next town?" Nan asked.

"No, for that will cause a parting between my wife and me, which I would not have for all the world," Monsieur Malateste said. "Therefore, Nan, God be with you."

"May your house be your hell and may your wife be your devil," Nan said.

Madame Malateste and her maid talked together.

"What will your ladyship have for your supper?" her maid asked.

"Whatever is splendid and costly," Madame Malateste replied.

Her maid exited, and the steward entered the room.

"Did your ladyship send for me?" the steward asked.

Madame Malateste said:

"Yes, for you, having been an old servant in my father's house, will be more diligent to observe and obey my commands.

"The first command is to go to the metropolitan city and there try all those who trade in vanities and see if they will give me credit, in case my husband should restrain his purse from me, and tell them that they may make my husband pay my debts.

"The next command is, I would have you rent for me a fine house in the city, for I intend to live there and not in this dull place where I see nobody but my husband, who spends his time in sneaking after his maid's tails, having no other employment."

"Tails" are buttocks.

Apparently, Madame Malateste was not having sex with her husband.

Madame Malateste continued:

"Besides, solitariness begets melancholy, and melancholy begets suspicion, and suspicion begets jealousy, so that my husband grows amorous with idleness, and jealous with melancholy. Thus he has the pleasure of variety, and I have the pain of jealousy.

"Therefore, be industrious in obeying my commands."

"I shall, madam," the steward said.

— 5.7 —

Mademoiselle Amour and her father, Monsieur Sensible, talked together.

"Good sir, conceal my passion, lest it become a scorn when once it is known," Mademoiselle Amour said. "For all rejected lovers are despised, as are those lovers who have some small returns of love; yet those faint affections triumph vaingloriously upon those who are strong and make them their slaves."

"Surely, child, thy affections shall not be divulged by me," Monsieur Sensible said. "I only wish thy passions were as silent in thy breast as on my tongue, as I wish that he whom thou love so much may lie as if dead and buried in thy memory."

"There's no way to bury love, unless it buries me," Mademoiselle Amour said.

— 5.8 —

Monsieur Malateste and Madame Malateste talked together.

"I hear, wife, that you are going to the metropolitan city," Monsieur Malateste said.

"Yes, husband, for I find myself much troubled with the spleen, and therefore I go to see if I can be cured," Madame Malateste said.

According to her words about the spleen, Madame Malateste was depressed and melancholic.

"Why, will the city cure the spleen?" Monsieur Malateste asked.

"Yes, for it is the only remedy, for melancholy must be diverted with divertissements: diversions," Madame Malateste said. "Besides, there in the city are the best physicians."

"I will send for some of the best and most famous physicians from thence, if you will stay," Monsieur Malateste said.

"By no means, for they will exact so much upon your importance that they will cost more money than their journey is worth," Madame Malateste said.

Because Monsieur Malateste had a high social status and much wealth, the physicians would overcharge him.

"But wife, it is my delight and profit to live in the country," Monsieur Malateste said. "Besides, I hate the city."

"And I hate the country," Madame Malateste said.

"But every good wife ought to conform herself to her husband's humors and will," Monsieur Malateste said.

"But husband, I say that I am no good wife," Madame Malateste said. "Therefore, I will follow my own humor."

Among other things, humors are desires and whims and moods.

Madame Malateste exited.

Alone, Monsieur Malateste said to himself, "I find there is no crossing her. She will have her will. She will do what she wants."

— 5.9 —

Monsieur Mari and Madame Soeur talked together. They were husband and wife.

"Wife, I have come to rob your cabinet of all the ribbons that are in it, for I have made a running match between Monsieur la Whip's nag and your brother's barbary horse, and your brother says that his horse shall not run unless you give him ribbons because he is persuaded that your favors will make his horse win," Monsieur Mari said.

In this society, the word "nag" did not necessarily mean a bad horse.

"Favors" are small gifts from ladies.

In medieval tournaments, a knight would wear his lady's favors as he competed.

"Those ribbons I have, you shall have, husband," Madame Soeur said. "But what will my brother say if his barbary horse should lose the race?"

"I asked him that question, and he answered that, if he lost, he would knock his barbary horse's brains out of his head," Monsieur Mari said.

"Where is my brother?" Madame Soeur asked.

"Why, he is with your father; and such a good companion he is today, and so merry, that your father is so fond of his company, in as much as he hangs about his neck like a new-married wife," Monsieur Mari said. "But I conceive the chief reason is that your brother seems to consent to marry the Lady Amour."

"I am glad of that with all my soul," Madame Soeur said.

"But, he says, if he does marry her, it must be by your persuasions," Monsieur Mari said.

"He shall not lack persuading if I can persuade him," Madame Soeur said.

"Come, wife, will you give me some ribbons?" Monsieur Mari asked.

"Yes, husband. I will go fetch them," Madame Soeur said.

"Nay, wife, I will go along with you," Monsieur Mari said.

— 5.10 —

Alone, Mademoiselle Amour, in a melancholy mood, said to herself, "Thoughts, cease to move and let my soul take rest, or let the damps of grief quench out life's flame."

Her father, Monsieur Sensible, entered the scene and said to her, "My dear child, do not pine away for love because I will get thee a handsomer man than Monsieur Frere."

"Sir, I am not so much in love with the attractiveness of his person as to dote so fondly thereon," Mademoiselle Amour replied.

She doted on him, but not because — or not just because — he was attractive.

"What makes you so in love with him, then?" Monsieur Sensible said. "For you have no great acquaintance with him."

They barely knew each other.

"Lovers can seldom give a reason for their passion," Mademoiselle Amour said. "Yet mine grew from your superlative praises; those praises drew my soul out at my ears to entertain his love. But since my soul misses what it seeks, it will not return, but leave my body empty to wander like a ghost, in gloomy sadness and midnight melancholy."

Monsieur Sensible said:

"I was mistaken about the subject I spoke about: The substance was false.

"Those praises were not current, so therefore lay them aside and fling them from thee."

"Current" means "generally accepted."

The word also means "legal tender."

Monsieur Sensible had been mistaken about Monsieur Frere when he had arranged a marriage for his daughter with him.

"I cannot, for they are minted and have love's stamp, and, being out, increases like to interest-money, and has become so vast a sum that I believe all praises — past, present, or what's to come or can be — are too few for his merits and too short of his worth," Mademoiselle Amour said.

In other words: The praises of Monsieur Frere are like money that has been lent out at interest and which therefore grows ever greater in value.

Money, when minted, is stamped, usually with the image of a sovereign.

"Rather than praise him, I wish that my tongue had been forever dumb," Monsieur Sensible said.

"O, don't wish that, but rather wish that I had been forever deaf," Mademoiselle Amour said.

She exited.

Alone, Monsieur Sensible said to himself, "My child is undone. She is destroyed."

— 5.11 —

Two servants of Monsieur Malateste talked together.

"My master looks so lean and pale that I fear he is in a consumption," the first servant said.

A consumption is a consuming disease that makes one lose weight.

"Indeed, he takes something to heart, whatever it is," the second servant said.

"I fear that he is jealous," the first servant said.

"He has reason because even if my lady does not cuckold him, she gives the world reason to think she does, for she is never without her gallants," the second servant said.

"There is a great difference between our lady who is dead, and this lady, " the first servant said.

Monsieur Malateste entered the room and asked, "Has my wife come home yet?"

"No, sir," the first servant said.

"I think it is about twelve of the clock," Monsieur Malateste said.

"It is past one, sir," the first servant said.

"If it is so late, I will sit up no longer watching for my wife's coming home, but I will go to bed because I am not very well," Monsieur Malateste said.

"You do not look well, sir," the first servant said.

"Indeed, I am sick," Monsieur Malateste replied.

— 5.12 —

Monsieur Frere entered the room that his sister, Madame Soeur, was in.

"Lord brother, what is the reason that you have come back so soon?" she asked. "Has your barbary horse run the race?"

"No," he answered.

"What are you doing here then?" she asked.

"I came to see you," he said.

"To see me?" she said. "Why, I shall give you no thanks because you left my husband behind you."

"I did not come for your thanks," he said. "I came to please myself."

"Please, brother, get thee gone, for thy face does not appear as honest as it used to appear," she said.

"I do not know how my face appears, but my heart is as it was: your faithful lover," he said.

"Heaven forbid you should relapse into your old disease," his sister said.

He replied:

"Let me tell you, sister, I am as I was, and I was as I am.

"That is, from the first time I saw you — since I came home from travel — I have been in love with you, and I must enjoy you; and if you will embrace my love with a free consent, so be it. If not, I'll force you to it."

In other words: I want to enjoy you sexually. If you will go to bed with me willingly, good. But if you won't, then I'll rape you.

"Heaven will never allow it, for it will instead cleave the earth and swallow you alive," his sister said.

Despite what she had said, Heaven remains inactive all too often.

Matthew 6:26 states, *"Behold the fowls of the air: for they sow not, neither do they reap, nor gather into barns; yet your heavenly Father feedeth them. Are ye not much better than they?"* (King James Version).

All of us have seen dead birds. Many of us have seen dead people.

"I don't care, as long as you are in my arms," he said, "but I will first test Heaven's power, and struggle with the deities."

He took her in his arms and carried her out.

His sister cried, "Help! Help! Murder! Murder!"

A more accurate cry would have been, "Help! Help! Rape! Rape!"

— 5.13 —

Monsieur Malateste, who was not well, and his wife, Madame Malateste, talked together.

"Wife, is this the way to cure melancholy?" Monsieur Malateste said. "To sit up all night at cards, and to lose five hundred pounds at a sitting? Or to stay out all night dancing and reveling?"

Madame Malateste answered:

"O, yes; for the doctors say there is nothing better than good company to employ the thoughts with (the doctors meant outward objects), otherwise the thoughts feed too much upon the body.

"Besides, they say that exercise is excellently good to open obstructions and to disperse the melancholy vapor, and the doctors say there is no exercise better than dancing because there are a great company who meet together, which adds pleasure to the labor."

"My other wife did not do this," Monsieur Malateste said.

"Therefore she died in her youth with melancholy," Madame Malateste said. "But I mean to live until and while I am old, if mirth and good company will keep me alive; and you should know that I am not so kind-hearted to kill myself to spare your purse or to please your humor."

She wanted to reach old age, and she wished to enjoy herself in old age (as well as now while she was young).

Madame Malateste exited, and her husband, sighing, followed her.

— 5.14 —

Madame Soeur had been raped by her brother, and she looked it.

Alone, she said to herself:

"Who will call to the gods for aid, since they do not assist those who are innocent, nor do they give protection to a virtuous life?

"Is piety of no use? Or is Heaven so obdurate that no holy prayers can enter Heaven-gates and no penitential tears can move the gods to pity?

"But O, my sorrows are too big for words, and all actions are too little for his punishment."

Monsieur Frere entered the room. His clothing was unbuttoned, and his sword was drawn in his hand.

"Sister, I must die, and therefore you must not live," he said, "for I cannot be without your company, although I would have your company in death and in the silent grave, where no love is made and no passion is known."

"It's welcome news," his sister said, "for if death does not come by your hand, my hand shall give a passage to life so it can exit my body."

"There is none so fit to act that part as I, who am so full of sin, lack nothing now except murder to make up measure," Monsieur Frere said.

He wanted to commit a full measure of sin. The only sin lacking was murder.

He gave his sister a mortal wound.

She said:

"Death, thou are my grief's reprieve, and will unload from my soul the heavy thoughts that miserable life throws on and sinks me to the earth.

"Brother, farewell; may all your crimes be buried in my grave and may my shame and yours never be known."

She cried out in pain and died.

Monsieur Frere said:

"Now that she is dead my mind is at rest, since I know no one can enjoy her in bed after me. But I will follow thee: I come, my mistress, wife, and sister all in one."

He fell upon the point of his sword, giving himself a mortal wound.

He lay close by his sister and put his arm over her, and then he said:

"You gods of love, if any gods there be, O hear my prayer! As we came both from one womb, so join our souls in the Elysium, and place our bodies in one tomb."

Elysium is the place in the Land of the Dead where the souls of good people go.

He cried out in pain and died.

His sister had recently been suffering from morning sickness. (See 1.5.)

— 5.15 —

Monsieur Malateste lay upon a couch, sick with a consumption. His friend Monsieur Fefy sat by him.

Madame Malateste entered the room.

"Wife, you are very unkind in that you will not come to see me now I am sick, nor will you do as much as send someone to find out how I am doing," Monsieur Malateste complained.

"I am loath to trouble you with unnecessary visits or impertinent questions," his wife replied.

"Is it unnecessary or impertinent to see a husband when he is sick?" Monsieur Malateste asked. "Or to ask how he is doing?"

"Yes, when their visits and questions can do them no good," his wife said. "But God be with you because I must be gone."

82

"What! Already?" Monsieur Malateste said.

"Yes. I fear that I have stayed too long, for I have appointed a meeting and it will be a dishonor for me to break my word," his wife said.

"But it will be more dishonor to be dancing when your husband is dying, lady," Monsieur Fefy said.

"What! Will you teach me?" Madame Malateste said. "Go tutor girls and boys, and not me."

She started to leave, and Monsieur Fefy moved as if he were going to stop her, but Monsieur Malateste said, "Let her go, friend, because her anger will disturb me."

Madame Malateste exited.

While actor John Barrymore (1882-1941) was on his deathbed in the hospital, his friend Gene Fowler telephoned Diana, Mr. Barrymore's daughter, who said, "I can't make it — I have an important appointment." Mr. Fowler replied, "So does your father," and hung up.

"I don't know what her anger does to you, but her neglect of you disturbs me, and for my part, I wonder how you can endure her," Monsieur Fefy said.

"Alas, how shall I help or remedy it?" Monsieur Malateste said. "But Heaven is just and punishes me for the neglectful way I treated my first wife, who was virtuous and kind."

"She was a sweet lady indeed," Monsieur Fefy said.

Monsieur Malateste said:

"O, she was! But I, devil as I was to treat her as I did, making her a slave to my whore and my frowns, and twisting all her virtues to a contrary sense because I mistook her patience for simplicity, her kindness for wantonness, her thrift for covetousness, her obedience for flattery, and her retired life for dull stupidity.

"And what with the grief to think how ill I treated her and grieving to see how ill this wife treats me, wasting my honor and estate, she has brought me into a consumption, as you see."

His new wife acted in such a way that everyone thought she was cuckolding him, and she wasted his money in card games and entertainments.

Monsieur Malateste continued:

"But when I am dead, as I cannot live long, I desire you, who are my executor, to let me be buried in the same tomb in which my first wife is laid.

"For it is a joy to me to think my dust shall be mixed with her pure ashes, for I had rather be in the grave with my first wife than live in a throne with my second.

"But I grow very sick, even to death; therefore, let me be moved from here."

Monsieur Malateste repented his sins before he died; Monsieur Frere did not repent his sins before he died.

— 5.16 —

Monsieur Pere and his son-in-law, Monsieur Mari, talked together.

"Son-in-law, did your brother say he was very ill?" Monsieur Pere asked.

"He said he had such a pain on his left side that he could not sit on his horse and was forced to return home again," Monsieur Mari said.

"May Heaven bless him, for my heart is so full of fears and worries, as if it did prognosticate some great misfortune to me," Monsieur Pere said.

The word "bless" means "protect."

"Pity, sir, don't be so dejected, nor look so pale," Monsieur Mari said. "I dare to assure you the news that his barbary horse has won the race will be a sufficient cataplasm to take away his stitch."

A cataplasm is a medicinal poultice.

A servant entered the room.

"How are my son and daughter?" Monsieur Pere asked.

"I think they are both well, sir," the servant answered.

"Why, you don't know, and yet you dwell in the same house with them?" Monsieur Pere said.

"No, indeed, not I, for I only saw my young master go towards my lady's lodging, but I did not follow to inquire of their healths for fear they should be angry, and think that I was bold," the servant said.

Madame Soeur's maid entered the room.

"Where is your lady?" Monsieur Pere asked.

"In her chamber, I think, sir," the maid answered.

"Do you only think so? Don't you know? It is a sign you don't wait on her very diligently," Monsieur Pere said.

"Why sir, I met my young master going to his sister's chamber and he sent me on an errand, and when I came back the outward doors were locked, so that I could not get in any ways," the maid said.

"The doors were locked, do you say?" Monsieur Mari asked.

"Yes, sir," the maid said.

"Let them be broken open," Monsieur Mari ordered.

"O, my fears foretell a miserable tragedy," Monsieur Pere said.

A servant broke the door open.

The servant, seeing the murdered couple, cried, "Murder! Murder!"

Monsieur Pere fell down dead from Takotsubo cardiomyopathy, which mimics a heart attack and is caused by a sudden great shock, at the sight of his dead children.

While the servant tried to recover life in the old man, Monsieur Mari ran to his murdered wife and fell to the ground and kissed her, and then he tore his hair and beat his breast, and, out of his wits, he rose hastily and grabbed the bloody sword so he could kill himself.

Servants grabbed and restrained him and tried to get the sword from his hand.

Monsieur Mari shouted:

"Villains, let go!

"She shall not wander in the silent shades without my company.

"Besides, my soul will crowd through multitudes of souls that flock to Charon's boat, to make an easy passage for her pure soul; therefore, let go!

"I command you as your master, let go!"

Charon is the ferryman who transports souls across a river to the Land of the Dead.

The servants continued to try to get the sword away from him.

More servants entered the room, and they carried out Monsieur Mari, who was still out of his wits and wanted to kill himself.

Monsieur Pere, who could not be revived, was carried out along with the bodies of his children.

Three servants entered the room.

"This is so strange an accident that hardly any story can mention the like," the first servant said.

"I wonder how they came to be murdered, the door being locked and no one inside but themselves," the second servant said. "If it had been thieves, they would have robbed them as well as murdered them."

"I believe my young master was the thief who did both rob and murder," the first servant said.

The young master — Monsieur Frere — had robbed his sister of her chastity.

Chastity includes ethical sex.

"Well, I could tell a story that I heard, listening one day at my lady's chamber-door; but I will not," the third servant said.

"Please tell it to us," the first servant said.

"No, I will not," the third servant said. "You shall excuse me at this time."

— 5.17 —

Monsieur Sensible and Mademoiselle Amour talked together.

"Daughter, I have come to bring you a medicine to take out the sting of love," Monsieur Sensible said.

"What is it, sir?" Mademoiselle Amour asked.

"Why, Monsieur Frere has most wickedly killed himself," Monsieur Sensible said.

She staggered.

"Although I cannot usher him to the grave, I'll follow him," Mademoiselle Amour said.

She fell down dead.

This was not a suicide.

Like Monsieur Pere, she had died from Takotsubo cardiomyopathy.

Monsieur Sensible called:

"Help! Help!

"For Heaven's sake, help!"

Some servants entered the room.

Monsieur Sensible continued:

"O, my child is dead! O, she is dead, she is dead! Carry her to her bed."

Monsieur Sensible and the servants, carrying his dead daughter, exited.

Two servants ran into the room from different directions and met each other.

"O, my lady is quite dead and past all cure, and her father, I think, will die, also," the first servant said.

The second servant said, "I am sure there is a sad, sad house today."

EPILOGUE

If subtle air, the conduit to each ear,

    Hearts' passion moved to draw a sadder tear

    From your squeezed [subjected to pressure] brains, on your pale cheeks to
lie,

    Distilled from every fountain of each eye;

    Our poetess has done her part, and you,

    To make it sadder, know this story's true;

    A plaudity [Applause] you'll give, if [you] think it fit,

    For none but [For everyone] will say this play is well writ [written].

    *The Lord Marquess of Newcastle wrote this Epilogue. The Lord Marquess of
Newcastle is William Cavendish, the husband of Margaret Cavendish."*

APPENDIX A: NOTES

— 1.1 —

The Luisa Tetrazzini anecdote is retold from this book:

Source: Nigel Douglas. *Legendary Voices*. London: Andre Deutsch Limited, 1992. Pp. 233-234.

— 1.5 —

For Your Information:

Among people who know they're pregnant, it's estimated about 1 in 8 pregnancies will end in miscarriage. Many more miscarriages happen before a person is even aware they're pregnant. Losing 3 or more pregnancies in a row (recurrent miscarriages) is uncommon and only affects around 1 in 100 women.

Source of Above: "Miscarriage: Overview." National Health Service (UK). Page last reviewed: 9 March 2022.
https://www.nhs.uk/conditions/miscarriage/

— 1.7 —

The Cicero Anecdote:

The scenario is this. It is the trial of Milo, accused of killing the infamous, wildly unpopular, colourful, controversial aristocrat Clodius (this is all late-Republican political meltdown stuff).

Cicero was defending Milo, but he himself was being interrogated by the prosecution.

The question came: What time did Clodius die?

Cicero answered: "Sero."

That, dear non Latinists, means "late"; and also "too late". The pun is, then, that Clodius died late in the day; but also he should have been got rid of ages ago.

Source: Charlotte Higgins, "Cicero was the funniest Roman, says Mary Beard." *Guardian* (UK). 3 April 2009

https://12ft.io/
proxy?q=https%3A%2F%2Fwww.theguardian.com%2Fculture%2Fcharlottehigginsbl

— 2.3 —

For Your Information:

Of the 33 ministers who make up [Boris] Johnson's new cabinet, 45% went to either Oxford or Cambridge university, while a further 24% attended Russell Group universities. Of all MPs in the House of Commons, 24% attended Oxford or Cambridge.

Johnson went to Eton college, and like every prime minister since 1937 who had attended university, except Gordon Brown, studied at Oxford.

Source: Amy Walker, "Two-thirds of Boris Johnson's cabinet went to private schools." *Guardian.* 25 July 2019

https://www.theguardian.com/education/2019/jul/25/two-thirds-of-boris-johnsons-cabinet-went-to-private-schools

— 2.3 —

1 VIRGIN
You say true; and as there is no prince that hath had the like good fortune as Alexander and Caesar, so none have had the like generosities as they had, which shows as if Fortune (when she dealt in good earnest, and not in mockery) measured her gifts by the largeness of the heart, and the liberality of the hand of those she gave to. And as for the death of those 40 two worthies, she had no hand in them, nor was she any way guilty thereof; for the gods distribute life and death without the help of Fortune.
(2.3.36-42)
Source of Above:
Cavendish, Margaret. *The Unnatural Tragedy*. Andrew Duxfield, editor. 2016. PDF. P. 17.

https://extra.shu.ac.uk/emls/iemls/renplays/
The%20Unnatural%20Tragedy.pdf

For Your Information:

Caesar's will was now produced and the people ordered that it be read at once. In it Octavian, the grandson of his sister, was adopted by Caesar. His gardens were given to the people as a place of recreation, and to every Roman still living in the city he gave seventy-five Attic drachmas.

Source of Above: Appian, *The Civil Wars*. Book 2. Chapter 143.
https://penelope.uchicago.edu/Thayer/E/Roman/Texts/Appian/Civil_Wars/2*.html#143

For Your Information:

Alexander was utterly generous regarding the rewards of men who distinguished themselves in battles and sieges. According to Diodorus, after the victories at Issus and Gaugamela donations of 3,000 talents were made, while for the conquest of Ecbatana jewels and 13,000 talents were distributed. According to Arrian, Greek allies who wished to repatriate were given 2,000 talents, while those who decided to stay after all received 3 talents each. Alexander was also generous towards veterans. According to Arrian, Macedonians who couldn't fight anymore due to old age or illness, received their salary and one extra talent, as well as the costs of the journey back home.

Source of Above: "Alexander the Great: a very competent expert in finances." Archeology Wiki. 30 November 2012
https://www.archaeology.wiki/blog/opinion/alexander-the-great-a-very-competent-expert-in-finances/

For Your Information:

Alexander most likely died from malaria or typhoid fever, which were rampant in ancient Babylon. The description of his final illness from the royal diaries is consistent with typhoid fever or malaria but is most characteristic of typhoid fever.

Source of Above: Burke A Cunha. "The death of Alexander the Great: malaria or typhoid fever?" National Library of Medicine. March 2004
Infect Dis Clin North Am. 2004 Mar;18(1):53-63.

doi: 10.1016/S0891-5520(03)00090-4.

https://pubmed.ncbi.nlm.nih.gov/15081504/

— **2.6** —

Faith, my brain is like Salisbury Plain today, where my thoughts run
races, having nothing to hinder their way, and my brain,
like Salisbury Plain, is so hard, as my thoughts, like the horse's heels,
leave no print behind. So as I have no wit today, for wit is the print and 5
mark of thoughts.

(2.16.2-6)

Source of Above:

Cavendish, Margaret. *The Unnatural Tragedy*. Andrew Duxfield, editor.
2016. PDF. P. 21.

https://extra.shu.ac.uk/emls/iemls/renplays/
The%20Unnatural%20Tragedy.pdf

For Your Information:

Westbury or Bratton White Horse is a hill figure on the escarpment of
Salisbury Plain, approximately 1.5 mi east of Westbury in Wiltshire,
England. Located on the edge of Bratton Downs and lying just below
an Iron Age hill fort, it is the oldest of several white horses carved in
Wiltshire.

[...]

Although it is the oldest of the Wiltshire white horses, the origin of
Westbury White Horse is obscure. [1] It is often claimed to
commemorate King Alfred's victory at the Battle of Ethandun in 878,
and while this is quite plausible, there is no trace of such a legend
before the second half of the 18th century. Perhaps more believable is
a theory that it was created at a much later date to commemorate this
early "English victory", particularly as King Alfred had a very strong
following in England from the 17th Century onwards, see for example
King Alfred's Tower.

Source of Above: "Westbury White Horse." Wikipedia

https://en.wikipedia.org/wiki/Westbury_White_Horse
For Your Information:

White horses have a special significance in the mythologies of cultures around the world. They are often associated with the sun chariot,[1] with warrior-heroes, with fertility (in both mare and stallion manifestations), or with an end-of-time saviour, but other interpretations exist as well. Both truly white horses and the more common grey horses, with completely white hair coats, were identified as "white" by various religious and cultural traditions.

Source of Above: "White horse symbolism." Wikipedia. Accessed 7 September 2022.
https://en.wikipedia.org/wiki/White_horses_in_mythology

— **2.6** —

The quotations from the *Iliad* are from my retelling of the epic poem:
Bruce, David. *Homer's* Iliad: *A Retelling in Prose.*
https://www.smashwords.com/books/view/264676
https://drive.google.com/file/d/18tiAjtd5a6Qil0FHIss2UpCEacizaij3/view?usp=sharing
https://davidbruceblog429065578.wordpress.com/ancient-literature-retellings-free-pdfs/

— **2.6** —

More information about Thucydides:

22. As to the speeches which were made either before or during the war, it was hard for me, and 1 for others who reported them to me, to recollect the exact words. I have therefore put into the mouth of each speaker the sentiments proper to the occasion, expressed as I thought he would be likely to express them, while at the same time I endeavoured, as nearly as I could, to give the general purport of what was actually said. [2] Of the events of the war I have not ventured to speak from any chance information, nor according to any notion of my own; I have described nothing but what I either saw myself, or learned from others of whom I made the most careful and particular enquiry. [3] The task was a laborious one, because eye-witnesses of the same occurrences gave different accounts of them, as they remembered or were interested in the actions of one side or the other. [4] And very likely the strictly historical character of my narrative may be disappointing to the ear. But if he who desires to have before his eyes a true picture of the events which have happened, and of the like events which may be expected to happen hereafter in the order of human things, shall pronounce what I have written to be useful, then I shall be satisfied. My history is an everlasting possession, not a prize composition which is heard and forgotten.

1 The speeches could not be exactly reported. Great pains taken to ascertain the truth about events.

Source of Above: *Thucydides translated into English; with introduction, marginal analysis, notes, and indices.* Volume 1. Thucydides. Benjamin Jowett. translator. Oxford. Clarendon Press. 1881.
http://www.perseus.tufts.edu/hopper/
text?doc=Perseus%3Atext%3A1999.04.0105%3Abook%3D1%3Achapter%3D22
More Information about Tacitus:

The Roman historian Cornelius Tacitus often fashioned speeches by a systematic ordering, where one speech repudiates the other. In this paper I will look closely at two sets of juxtaposed speeches. The first set, from the Agricola, includes speeches by Calgacus, the chieftain of the Caledonians in Britain, and Gnaeus Julius Agricola, Roman governor of Britain from 78 to 87 A.O. (Agr. 30-34). The second set, from the Annales, consists of those by Boudicca, the widowed queen of the Iceni in Britain, and Suetonius Paulinus, the Roman governor of Britain from 58 to 61 A.O. (Ann. 14.35-36).

Source of Above: Thomas J. Santa Maria Jr., "The Speeches of Boudicca and Calgacus: Tacitus's Unified Text of Imperial Critique." *New England Classical Journal.* Volume 40 Issue 2 Pages 123-134. May 2013.
https://crossworks.holycross.edu/cgi/
viewcontent.cgi?article=1296&context=necj

— **2.6** —

An excerpt from Book 2 of Plato's *Republic*:

"Neither must we admit at all," said I, "that gods war with gods 133 and plot against one another and contend—for it is not true either—[378c] if we wish our future guardians to deem nothing more shameful than lightly to fall out with one another; still less must we make battles of gods and giants the subject for them of stories and embroideries, 134 and other enmities many and manifold of gods and heroes toward their kith and kin. But if there is any likelihood of our persuading them that no citizen ever quarrelled with his fellow-citizen and that the very idea of it is an impiety, [378d] that is the sort of thing that ought rather to be said by their elders, men and women, to children from the beginning and as they grow older, and we must compel the poets to keep close to this in their compositions. But Hera's fetterings 135 by her son and the hurling out of heaven of Hephaestus by his father when he was trying to save his mother from a beating, and the battles of the gods 136 in Homer's verse are things that we must not admit into our city either wrought in allegory 137 or without allegory. For the young are not able to distinguish what is and what is not allegory, but whatever opinions are taken into the mind at that age are wont to prove [378e] indelible and unalterable. For which reason, maybe, we should do our utmost that the first stories that they hear should be so composed as to bring the fairest lessons of virtue to their ears."

Source of Above: Plato. *Plato in Twelve Volumes*, Vols. 5 & 6 translated by Paul Shorey. Cambridge, MA, Harvard University Press; London, William Heinemann Ltd. 1969.

http://www.perseus.tufts.edu/hopper/
text?doc=Perseus%3Atext%3A1999.01.0168%3Abook%3D2#note137

— **2.6** —

The translation of Tacitus is from this book:

Tacitus. *The Annuals of Imperial Rome*. Trans. Michael Grant. Penguin. 1973.

https://www.google.com/books/edition/
The_Annals_of_Imperial_Rome/
bzHAm7wZM-0C?hl=en&gbpv=1&bsq=fighting%20as%20an%20ordinary%20pers

— 2.6 —

An excerpt from Emperor Claudius' "Letter to the Alexandrian Embassy":

But I announce frankly that, unless you put a stop to this (80) destructive, relentless rage against each other, I shall be forced to show what a benevolent leader is when turned toward righteous rage. For this I yet again still bear witness that Alexandrines, on the one hand, behave gently and kindly with the Judeans, the inhabitants of the same city from a long time ago, (85) and not be disrespectful of the customs used in the ritual of their god, but let them use their customs as in the time of the god Sebastos even as I myself, after hearing both sides, have confirmed [...]

The letter was in part about peace between Greeks and Jews riots in the city and called for. The letter also warned Jews not to bring more Jews into the city.

Source of Above Quotation: Bruce C. Jones, "Emperor Claudius' Letter to the Alexandrian Embassy." 3/6/2015.

http://www.bricecjones.com/blog/emperor-claudius-letter-to-the-alexandrian-embassy

Claudius is named the fifth best Roman Emperor in this list:

"Top 10 Greatest Emperors of Ancient Rome." Last updated: August 30, 2022 by Saugat Adhikari. Ancient History Lists.

https://www.ancienthistorylists.com/rome-history/top-10-greatest-emperors-ancient-rome/

— 2.6 —

More Information About Giordano Bruno:

On 17 February 1600, in the Campo de' Fiori (a central Roman market square), with his "tongue imprisoned because of his wicked words", he was hung upside down naked before finally being burned at the stake.[58][59] His ashes were thrown into the Tiber river.

All of Bruno's works were placed on the Index Librorum Prohibitorum in 1603. The inquisition cardinals who judged Giordano Bruno were Cardinal Bellarmino (Bellarmine), Cardinal Madruzzo (Madruzzi), Camillo Cardinal Borghese (later Pope Paul V), Domenico Cardinal Pinelli, Pompeio Cardinal Arrigoni, Cardinal Sfondrati, Pedro Cardinal De Deza Manuel and Cardinal Santorio (Archbishop of Santa Severina, Cardinal-Bishop of Palestrina).[60]

The measures taken to prevent Bruno continuing to speak have resulted in his becoming a symbol for free thought and speech in present-day Rome, where an annual memorial service takes place close to the spot where he was executed.[61]

Source of Above: "Giordano Bruno." Wikipedia. Accessed 13 September 2022

https://en.wikipedia.org/wiki/Giordano_Bruno

— **2.6** —

For More Information:

Depictions of Nero as notorious are "based on a source narrative that is partisan," Thorsten Opper, a curator in the Greek and Roman division of the British Museum, told me recently. [...] Descriptions of Nero as unhinged and licentious belong to a rhetorical tradition of personal attack that flourished in the Roman courtroom. Opper told me, "They had a term for it—vituperatio, or 'vituperation,' which meant that you could say anything about your opponent. You can really invent all manner of things just to malign that character. And that is exactly the kind of language and stereotypes we find in the source accounts."

Source: Rebecca Mead," How Nasty Was Nero, Really?" *The New Yorker*.7 June 2021

The notorious emperor appears to have been the subject of a smear campaign.

https://www.newyorker.com/magazine/2021/06/14/how-nasty-was-nero-really

— 2.7 —

Syphilis: Cure

The first modern breakthrough in syphilis treatment was the development of Salvarsan, which was available as a drug in 1910. In the mid-1940s, industrialized production of penicillin finally brought about an effective and accessible cure for the disease.

Source of Above: "Mercury, Marriage, and Magic Bullets." Text and selections by Maija Anderson, Director, Curatorial Services. Historical Collections and Archives. Oregon Health & Science University.

https://www.ohsu.edu/historical-collections-archives/mercury-marriage-and-magic-bullets

— 3.9 —

Information about death and the early American colonists and the Thomas anecdote are retold from this book:

Chappell, Helen. *The Chesapeake Book of the Dead: Tombstones, Epitaphs, Histories, Reflections, and Oddments of the Region.* Baltimore, MD: The Johns Hopkins University Press, 1999. Pp. 27, 31.

— 4.3 —

For Your Information:

Many of the kings and queens of the Spanish Habsburg dynasty, which ruled across Europe from the 16th to the start of the 18th century, had a distinctive facial deformity: an elongated jaw that later became known as the "Habsburg jaw." Now, a new study suggests this facial feature was likely the result of centuries of inbreeding.

"The Habsburg dynasty was one of the most influential in Europe," lead author Roman Vilas, a professor of genetics at the University of Santiago de Compostela, said in a statement. But the dynasty "became renowned for inbreeding, which was its eventual downfall."

That is because the royal bloodline of the dynasty's Spanish branch ended in 1700 with the death of King Charles II, who couldn't produce an heir, likely as a result of inbreeding, according to a previous Live

Science report. But it was unclear if their tendency to inbreed was also written on their faces.

Source of Above: Yasemin Saplakoglu. "Inbreeding Caused the Distinctive 'Habsburg Jaw' of 17th Century Royals That Ruled Europe." Live Science. 2 December 2019

https://www.livescience.com/habsburg-jaw-inbreeding.html

— 4.6 —

The Jenny Thompson anecdote is retold from this book:

Christina Lessa, *Women Who Win* (New York: Universe Publishing, 1998), p. 75.

— 4.7 —

For Your Information:

Despite billions of years of cooling, our planet still has about half of the heat it was born with. Earth may have formed more than 4.5 billion years ago, but it's still cooling. A new study reveals that only about half of our planet's internal heat stems from natural radioactivity. The rest is primordial heat left over from when Earth first coalesced from a hot ball of gas, dust, and other material.

Source: Sid Perkins, "Earth Still Retains Much of Its Original Heat." Science.org. 17 July 2011

https://www.science.org/content/article/earth-still-retains-much-its-original-heat

— 4.7 —

The fart-sound anecdote is quoted word for word from this post:

Source: not_doing_that, "How did you accidentally kill the mood during consensual sex? And if you were able to salvage it, how did you?" Reddit. AskWomen. 15 May 2022

https://www.reddit.com/r/AskWomen/comments/uq5u4i/how_did_you_accidentally_kill_the_mood_during/

The Redditor who posted the anecdote in answer to the question is Justcameheretovote.

— 4.7 —

The John Custis and Fidelia Custis anecdotes are retold from this book:

Chappell, Helen. *The Chesapeake Book of the Dead: Tombstones, Epitaphs, Histories, Reflections, and Oddments of the Region*. Baltimore, MD: The Johns Hopkins University Press, 1999. Pp. 11-12.

— 5.15 —

The John Barrymore anecdote is retold from this book:

Source: H. Allen Smith, *Life and Legend of Gene Fowler* (New York: William Morrow and Co., 1977), p. 256.

— 5.16 & 5.17 —

Monsieur Pere dies suddenly in 5.16. Mademoiselle Amour dies of a broken heart in 5.17. Is this possible in real life?

For Your Information:

How can grief imitate a heart attack?

Broken heart syndrome is also called Takotsubo cardiomyopathy, named after the Japanese physician who identified it. It occurs in response to sudden emotional stress — particularly grief — and is more common in women than in men.

"Broken heart syndrome is probably caused by hormonal factors and an artery that spasms," explains cardiologist Marc Gillinov, MD. "It can imitate a heart attack, but heart attacks are caused by a blood clot in the arteries."

For reasons that are not well understood, a person will experience a huge surge of adrenaline that can stimulate a heart attack. The heart muscle stops contracting, and it will appear to be a heart attack, even when an electrocardiogram is performed.

Most of the time, when the spasms relaxes and blood flow resumes, the heart failure will usually resolve. If the heart failure doesn't improve, it could cause death in extremely rare circumstances.

Source of Above: "Can You Die of a Broken Heart? — And Other Emotional Questions." The Cleveland Clinic. 12 February 2020

99

Also for Your Information:

Dying of a "broken heart" may sound like it's coming from the pages of a book, but it is possible. You might associate a broken heart with mental health, but it can take its toll physically as well. This is known as "broken heart syndrome." It is brought on by stressful circumstances, like the death of a loved one. Cardiologist Tim Martin, MD, UnityPoint Health says it needs proper diagnosis and treatment just like any other cardiovascular diagnosis.

What is "Broken Heart Syndrome?"

According to the American Heart Association (AHA), broken heart syndrome, or takotsubo cardiomyopathy, is a reaction your heart has to a surge of stress hormones caused by an emotionally stressful event. Broken heart syndrome causes the heart to stop operating normally, resulting in heart failure. During these situations, the body releases an increase of hormones, which temporarily paralyzes your heart and limits its standard functionality.

"This syndrome is unique in that it can develop in anyone, even someone who is healthy by all other standards," Dr. Martin says.

The following are examples of high-stress situations that might trigger broken heart syndrome.

- Death of a loved one
- Bankruptcy
- Being fired from a job
- Public speaking
- Divorce
- Terminal medical diagnosis

Source of Above:

UnityPoint Health. "Can You Really Die From a Broken Heart?" 2022 https://www.unitypoint.org/livewell/article.aspx?id=a7f06d29-de06-4343-bfef-ebb12fc667bd

APPENDIX B: SHEFFIELD HALLAM UNIVERSITY STUDENT EDITIONS

The Sheffield Hallam University student editions I have looked at are good work and should be made available publicly, perhaps at Kindle Desktop Publishing or draft2create.com.

https://extra.shu.ac.uk/emls/iemls/resources.html

Text collections

Modern-spelling editions of Cavendish circle plays:

Jane Cavendish and Elizabeth Brackley, The Concealed Fancies, ed. Daniel Cadman (2015).

https://extra.shu.ac.uk/emls/iemls/renplays/ConcealedFancies.pdf

Margaret Cavendish, The Unnatural Tragedy, ed. Andrew Duxfield (2016).

https://extra.shu.ac.uk/emls/iemls/renplays/
The%20Unnatural%20Tragedy.pdf

"Early Stuart Libels: an edition of poetry from manuscript sources." Ed. Alastair Bellany and Andrew McRae. *Early Modern Literary Studies* Text Series I (2005).

http://purl.oclc.org/emls/texts/libels/

Edited modern-spelling etexts of Renaissance plays, prepared in connection with the *Editing a Renaissance Play* module of Sheffield Hallam University's MA in English Studies:

Anonymous, The Fatal Marriage, edited by Andrew Duxfield (2004).

https://extra.shu.ac.uk/emls/iemls/renplays/fatalindex.html

Anonymous, Lust's Dominion, edited by Mary Ellen Cacheado (2005). This text was used for the *Lust's Dominion* scenes in a 2008 episode of Channel 4's Peep Show.

https://extra.shu.ac.uk/emls/iemls/renplays/lustsdominion.htm

Anonymous, The Tragedy of Claudius Tiberius Nero, edited by Sharon McDonnell (2004).

https://extra.shu.ac.uk/emls/iemls/renplays/ctneroindex.html

Anonymous, The Tragedy of Nero, edited by Tracey Siddle (2004).

https://extra.shu.ac.uk/emls/iemls/renplays/tragedyofnero.htm

Anonymous, Two Lamentable Tragedies, edited by Gemma Leggott (2011).

https://www.google.com/
search?client=safari&rls=en&q=renplays%2FTwo+Lamentable+Tragedies+ed+

A pdf downloads when you click on the link on the website.

Anonymous, A Warning for Fair Women, edited by Gemma Leggott (2011).

https://www.google.com/
search?client=safari&rls=en&q=renplays%2FA+Warning+for+Fair+Women+V

A pdf downloads when you click on the link on the website.

Samuel Daniel, The Tragedy of Cleopatra, edited by Lucy Knight (2011).

https://extra.shu.ac.uk/emls/iemls/renplays/cleopatra.html

J.W. Gent's The Valiant Scot, edited by Pat Griffin (2007).

https://extra.shu.ac.uk/emls/iemls/renplays/valiantscot/
contents.htm

David Bruce's retelling of J.W. Gent's *The Valiant Scot* is available here:

https://www.smashwords.com/books/view/1163699

Richard Brome, The City Wit, edited by Katherine Wilkinson (2004). This text formed the basis for the 2007 production of the play by the Arts Academy, University of Ballarat.

https://extra.shu.ac.uk/emls/iemls/renplays/witindex.htm

Richard Brome, The Queen's Exchange, edited by Richard Wood (2005).

https://extra.shu.ac.uk/emls/iemls/renplays/qexchcontents.htm

Jasper Fisher, Fuimus Troes, edited by Chris Butler (2007).

https://extra.shu.ac.uk/emls/iemls/renplays/fuimustroes.htm

John Ford, The Queen, edited by Tim Seccombe (2008).

https://extra.shu.ac.uk/emls/iemls/renplays/queencontents.htm

David Bruce's retelling of John Ford's *The Queen* is available here:

https://www.smashwords.com/books/view/930049

Thomas Heywood, The Rape of Lucrece, edited by Chris Bailey (2009).

https://extra.shu.ac.uk/emls/iemls/renplays/rapelucrece/
contents.html

Gervase Markham and Lewis Machin, The Dumb Knight, edited by Kris Towse (2009).

https://extra.shu.ac.uk/emls/iemls/renplays/dumbknight.htm

Thomas May, The Tragedy of Agrippina, edited by Lyndsey Clarke (2003).

https://extra.shu.ac.uk/emls/iemls/renplays/mayindex.html

Thomas Rawlins, The Rebellion, edited by Amy Lockwood (2006).

https://extra.shu.ac.uk/emls/iemls/renplays/rawlreb.htm

Nathaniel Richards, The Tragedy of Messalina, the Roman Empress, edited by Samantha Gibbs (2004).

https://extra.shu.ac.uk/emls/iemls/renplays/
mess%20contents%20page.htm

George Wilkins, The Miseries of Enforced Marriage, edited by Rhiannon O'Grady (2002).

https://extra.shu.ac.uk/emls/iemls/renplays/miseries.htm

Individual etexts
John Spencer Hill. John Milton: Poet, Priest and Prophet. A Study of Divine Vocation in Milton's Poetry and Prose.
Romuald I. Lakowski,"A Bibliography of Thomas More's Utopia."
https://extra.shu.ac.uk/emls/01-2/lakomore.html
Romuald I. Lakowski. Sir Thomas More and the Art of Dialogue. Ph.D. Diss. U of British Columbia, Fall 1993.
https://extra.shu.ac.uk/emls/iemls/work/chapters/lakowski.html
R.G. Siemens, "Milton's Works and Life: Select Studies and Resources."
Early Modern Literary Studies, iEMLS Postprint
http://purl.oclc.org/emls/iemls/postprint/CCM2Biblio.html

Originally published in Dennis Danielson (ed.). *The Cambridge Companion to Milton.* 2nd ed. Cambridge, 1999. Pp. 268-90.

APPENDIX C: ABOUT THE AUTHOR

It was a dark and stormy night. Suddenly a cry rang out, and on a hot summer night in 1954, Josephine, wife of Carl Bruce, gave birth to a boy — me. Unfortunately, this young married couple allowed Reuben Saturday, Josephine's brother, to name their first-born. Reuben, aka "The Joker," decided that Bruce was a nice name, so he decided to name me Bruce Bruce. I have gone by my middle name — David — ever since.

Being named Bruce David Bruce hasn't been all bad. Bank tellers remember me very quickly, so I don't often have to show an ID. It can be fun in charades, also. When I was a counselor as a teenager at Camp Echoing Hills in Warsaw, Ohio, a fellow counselor gave the signs for "sounds like" and "two words," then she pointed to a bruise on her leg twice. Bruise Bruise? Oh yeah, Bruce Bruce is the answer!

Uncle Reuben, by the way, gave me a haircut when I was in kindergarten. He cut my hair short and shaved a small bald spot on the back of my head. My mother wouldn't let me go to school until the bald spot grew out again.

Of all my brothers and sisters (six in all), I am the only transplant to Athens, Ohio. I was born in Newark, Ohio, and have lived all around Southeastern Ohio. However, I moved to Athens to go to Ohio University and have never left.

At Ohio U, I never could make up my mind whether to major in English or Philosophy, so I got a bachelor's degree with a double major in both areas, then I added a Master of Arts degree in English and a Master of Arts degree in Philosophy. Yes, I have my MAMA degree.

Currently, and for a long time to come (I eat fruits and veggies), I am spending my retirement writing books such as *Nadia Comaneci: Perfect 10*, *The Funniest People in Comedy*, *Homer's* Iliad: *A Retelling in Prose*, and *William Shakespeare's* Hamlet: *A Retelling in Prose*.

If all goes well, I will publish one or two books a year for the rest of my life. (On the other hand, a good way to make God laugh is to tell Her your plans.)

By the way, my sister Brenda Kennedy writes romances such as *A New Beginning* and *Shattered Dreams*.

APPENDIX D: SOME BOOKS BY DAVID BRUCE

Retellings of a Classic Work of Literature

Arden of Faversham*: A Retelling*

Ben Jonson's The Alchemist: *A Retelling*

Ben Jonson's The Arraignment, or Poetaster: *A Retelling*

Ben Jonson's Bartholomew Fair: *A Retelling*

Ben Jonson's The Case is Altered: *A Retelling*

Ben Jonson's Catiline's Conspiracy: *A Retelling*

Ben Jonson's The Devil is an Ass: *A Retelling*

Ben Jonson's Epicene: *A Retelling*

Ben Jonson's Every Man in His Humor: *A Retelling*

Ben Jonson's Every Man Out of His Humor: *A Retelling*

Ben Jonson's The Fountain of Self-Love, or Cynthia's Revels: *A Retelling*

Ben Jonson's The Magnetic Lady, or Humors Reconciled: *A Retelling*

Ben Jonson's The New Inn, or The Light Heart: *A Retelling*

Ben Jonson's Sejanus' Fall: *A Retelling*

Ben Jonson's The Staple of News: *A Retelling*

Ben Jonson's A Tale of a Tub: *A Retelling*

Ben Jonson's Volpone, or the Fox: *A Retelling*

Christopher Marlowe's Complete Plays: Retellings

Christopher Marlowe's Dido, Queen of Carthage: *A Retelling*

Christopher Marlowe's Doctor Faustus: *Retellings of the 1604 A-Text and of the 1616 B-Text*

Christopher Marlowe's Edward II: *A Retelling*

Christopher Marlowe's The Massacre at Paris: *A Retelling*

Christopher Marlowe's The Rich Jew of Malta: *A Retelling*

Christopher Marlowe's Tamburlaine, Parts 1 and 2: *Retellings*

Dante's Divine Comedy: *A Retelling in Prose*

Dante's Inferno: *A Retelling in Prose*

Dante's Purgatory: *A Retelling in Prose*

Dante's Paradise: *A Retelling in Prose*

The Famous Victories of Henry V: *A Retelling*

From the Iliad *to the* Odyssey: *A Retelling in Prose of Quintus of Smyrna's* Posthomerica

George Chapman, Ben Jonson, and John Marston's Eastward Ho! *A Retelling*

George Peele's The Arraignment of Paris: *A Retelling*

George Peele's The Battle of Alcazar: *A Retelling*

George Peele's David and Bathsheba, and the Tragedy of Absalom: *A Retelling*

George Peele's Edward I: *A Retelling*

George Peele's The Old Wives' Tale: *A Retelling*

George-a-Greene: *A Retelling*

The History of King Leir: *A Retelling*

Homer's Iliad: *A Retelling in Prose*

Homer's Odyssey: *A Retelling in Prose*

J.W. Gent.'s The Valiant Scot: *A Retelling*

Jason and the Argonauts: A Retelling in Prose of Apollonius of Rhodes' Argonautica

John Ford: Eight Plays Translated into Modern English

John Ford's The Broken Heart: *A Retelling*

John Ford's The Fancies, Chaste and Noble: *A Retelling*

John Ford's The Lady's Trial: *A Retelling*

John Ford's The Lover's Melancholy: *A Retelling*

John Ford's Love's Sacrifice: *A Retelling*

John Ford's Perkin Warbeck: *A Retelling*

John Ford's The Queen: *A Retelling*

John Ford's 'Tis Pity She's a Whore: *A Retelling*

John Lyly's Campaspe: *A Retelling*

John Lyly's Endymion, The Man in the Moon: *A Retelling*

John Lyly's Galatea: *A Retelling*

John Lyly's Love's Metamorphosis: *A Retelling*

John Lyly's Midas: *A Retelling*

John Lyly's Mother Bombie: *A Retelling*

John Lyly's Sappho and Phao: *A Retelling*

John Lyly's The Woman in the Moon: *A Retelling*

John Webster's The White Devil: *A Retelling*

King Edward III: *A Retelling*

Mankind: *A Medieval Morality Play* (A Retelling)

Margaret Cavendish's The Unnatural Tragedy: *A Retelling*

The Merry Devil of Edmonton: *A Retelling*

Robert Greene's Friar Bacon and Friar Bungay: *A Retelling*

The Summoning of Everyman: *A Medieval Morality Play* (A Retelling)

The Taming of a Shrew: *A Retelling*

Tarlton's Jests: A Retelling

Thomas Middleton's A Chaste Maid in Cheapside: *A Retelling*

Thomas Middleton's Women Beware Women: *A Retelling*

Thomas Middleton and Thomas Dekker's The Roaring Girl: *A Retelling*

Thomas Middleton and William Rowley's The Changeling: *A Retelling*

The Trojan War and Its Aftermath: Four Ancient Epic Poems

Virgil's Aeneid: *A Retelling in Prose*

William Shakespeare's 5 Late Romances: Retellings in Prose

William Shakespeare's 10 Histories: Retellings in Prose

William Shakespeare's 11 Tragedies: Retellings in Prose

William Shakespeare's 12 Comedies: Retellings in Prose